My Peeping Tom

A Small-Town Shifter Romance

Shelley Munro

My Highland Mate

Print ISBN: 978-1-99-106303-8
Digital ISBN: 978-0-473-34714-7

Editor: Mary Moran

Cover: Killion Group Inc.

Munro Press, New Zealand.

First Munro Press electronic publication Mar 2016

First Munro Press print publication Oct 2022

For Paul.

Introduction

Seduction is a matter of life or death...hers.

The residents of Middlemarch have a nickname for reporter Tomasine Brooks. They call her Peeping Tom and refuse to answer her questions about the mysterious black cats spotted in the vicinity. To them she's an outsider—the enemy—who has no place in their close-knit shifter community.

Tomasine is determined to find a safe place to settle but earning the locals' trust seems impossible. In desperation, she decides to seduce the sexy Felix Mitchell into giving away Middlemarch's secrets because it's a matter of life or death...hers.

From the moment feline shifter Felix Mitchell crashes into Tomasine outside the post office he desires her with an urgency that makes him suspect they are fated mates. When they are together the connection is hot, the sex is spicy and she makes him happy, but Tomasine is close-mouthed about her past—a past that can threaten their future together.

Chapter 1

Seduction Plan

Tomasine Brooks glanced up from her research notes as Gina entered the cramped living room of the house they rented in the country town of Middlemarch. After stacking her papers neatly on the pitted tabletop, she stood and navigated her way from the dinette area with its small table and three mismatched chairs. In the lounge, she reached over the faded green couch to pick up the remote for the television. She stabbed the power button, turning off the news and glanced back at her foster daughter—or cousin as she was introduced to anyone who asked.

"Is Sylvie settled?"

The teenager's lips quirked up at the corners and not a fraction farther. "I had to read her three stories before she dropped off but yeah. She's fast asleep now, Tom."

Tomasine wished the sixteen-year-old would smile without restraint and act her age. Instead, old eyes that had witnessed too much peered from her round face. She sighed inwardly. Not surprising. It was difficult for them all. Constantly looking over one's shoulder tended to kill anything but the need for survival. "You have my cell phone number, right?"

Gina's shoulders shifted in a gesture of irritation. "For the third time, yes, but I don't know what good it will do with Middlemarch's patchy reception. I had to ring you from the school toilets the other day. I couldn't get a dial tone anywhere else." She scowled at Tomasine, forestalling her next careful-parent instruction before she could voice her anxiety-filled advice. "And I won't answer the door or let any strangers inside. Either male or female," the teenager finished in an indignant rush.

"Just call me paranoid." Tomasine kept her tone light. She thought they were safe here in Middlemarch, but there was always a chance they'd been followed. Her stomach lurched at the idea of capture. *Never.*

She'd die first.

Her hand tightened to a fist at her side. Probably what the next lot of assassins intended to do, should they catch up with them. Kill them. They'd have to because Tomasine refused to set foot on African soil again while that creature ruled. She forced away the ubiquitous unease and rolled her shoulders to unwind the kinks.

Nerves.

Her morose thoughts fed from her anxiety. Felix Mitchell would attend the barn dance tonight. The male was tall. Dark. Sexy. All traits she admired in a man, qualities that made her look twice. Not that she was looking—after her husband's betrayal, she'd never trust a male again. However, if she were to go ahead with her plan, she needed to approach him.

4

Apprehension churned her stomach and the snack she'd eaten earlier sloshed around uneasily. Was Felix honest? Was Middlemarch the haven she so desperately needed for Sylvie, Gina and herself? A place for the girls to go to school and have a normal life—that was the question.

Gina jerked her head in the direction of the bottle of perfume bottle Tomasine had brought from the bedroom. "I suppose you want me to spray that godawful perfume all over you again." Gina picked up the bottle and strode across the stained beige carpet to stand beside her. The teenager towered over her five-feet-four frame, making Tomasine feel like the child.

"Are you sure this is a good idea?" Gina asked. "Once you put your plan into action, you'll have to see it through. Remember what you said about sex being a last resort."

Tomasine groaned aloud. "I knew I shouldn't have discussed the plan with you. It was a moment of weakness caused by that glass of wine. You're a teenager and shouldn't be thinking about sex let alone discussing it."

"I have needs," Gina said in a lofty voice.

"Needs," Tomasine echoed in horror. That was all she needed right now. They were on the run, trying to evade the assassins hired by the clan, she was trying to find them a safe place to live and Gina's libido decided to kick-start way too early. The girl was only sixteen. "Well, you can stuff those needs right back in the box where they came from, miss. I don't have time for a curious teenager." She raised her arms above her head. "Spray."

"Oh, Tom! I didn't mean I was going out on the town trolling for sex. That would make me a slut."

A fine mist of spray hit Tomasine in the face and she glared at Gina's innocent expression. Dammit, she wasn't a slut either. This was survival. She must follow through on this plan because she'd exhausted every other idea. A sneeze exploded, and when she swiped at the watery tears on her cheeks, she caught the teenager's smirk. Instantly her trepidation lightened. The wretch was teasing. It was such a normal teenage reaction she wanted to giggle in return.

"You do know about sex, right? Do I need to give you the talk?" Although she'd taken Gina under her wing, the girl was close-mouthed when it came to her family and past. Tomasine couldn't blame her since she hated to discuss her family, her husband...

"Don't worry," Gina said airily. She circled Tomasine and efficiently sprayed her from head to toe with perfume. "I'm not going to do anything to jeopardize our safety. But I can still look." Her hazel eyes shut and a soft smile played across her lips.

It was so uncharacteristic that Tomasine stared in shock. For an instant the girl appeared adult, then she blinked and Gina's familiar chubby face came into focus. "I guess looking can't hurt. We all need something to look forward to each day." Something in the girl's expression made her prod a bit harder. "Is there someone in particular?"

"Leo Mitchell," Gina said. "That man is a babe. His butt—"

"Enough." Tomasine held up her hand and pulled a face of mock alarm. Thoughts of the Mitchell brothers made her uncomfortable. Her pulse rate picked up and uneasiness and—blast it—arousal assailed her with vengeance. Part of it was because of her plan but the rest—the unknown factor—worried her more. An omen? The hairs at the scruff of her neck prickled and the sensation spread downward to catch at her breasts. She dragged in a sharp breath, riding out the needy ache caused by the friction of her nipples against the bodice of her dress.

She knew there were shapeshifters living in Middlemarch—she could smell the difference in the inhabitants. But she couldn't tell if this was a safe community. After two years of traveling the world, she needed to stop running, to find a safe place for her daughter Sylvie and for Gina. They both deserved a normal childhood full of love and security.

During the last two months, her attempts to get closer to the locals had failed dismally. In hindsight, passing herself off as a reporter hadn't been the wisest course but it was too late now. She was stuck with the cover and made a reasonable living writing fluff pieces for the paper in Dunedin. Apart from writing the one story about the local black panther sightings...

Now that had been a mistake.

"One look at Leo Mitchell's butt is not enough," Gina said. "I can't promise not to sneak another glance. Allow me one guilty pleasure."

Tomasine sighed, secretly glad of the distraction. Sometimes she felt as though she were talking to a contemporary, which was why sex had come up when it shouldn't have entered the discussion at all. "I don't suppose looking can hurt."

"No, it's the touching that gets you into trouble," Gina shot back.

She grimaced at Gina. Once again she regretted running her plan past the teenager. "Don't remind me." Now she was about to take the last steps in her plan to seduce Felix Mitchell and she wondered if she were about to make the biggest mistake of her life. A snort emerged at the anxious thought.

Oh yeah. Too late for that. Nothing she did would ever top trusting Bernard Lerfervre enough to take him as husband and mate. Her mouth firmed as she collected her bag and slung it over her shoulder. This plan had to work.

"How do I look? Will Felix Mitchell take the bait?" Tomasine did a slow twirl, the full sea-green skirt lifting in a whisper-soft rustle against her thighs. The fabric stopped above her knee—in fact the whole outfit was too abbreviated for her liking. It felt as if one full breath would make her pop right out of the bodice.

She reminded herself to save the heavy breathing until she snared Felix Mitchell and corralled him somewhere private. At that stage, it wouldn't matter if her bare breasts popped into prominence.

It could help her cause.

Earlier, she'd arranged her dark hair in a complicated twist, leaving her neck and shoulders bare. Beneath the breath-restricting dress, she wore wispy green panties and sheer flesh-colored stockings—the kind that stayed up without a garter belt.

"Felix Mitchell would need to be deaf and blind to miss you," Gina said. "I don't think any of the Mitchell brothers are short in the brains department. A brain and a sexy butt. Be still my heart." Gina patted the left-hand side of her chest.

"Go and watch the cartoon channel," Tomasine suggested. "Something wholesome, but finish your homework first."

"Sure, Tom. I'm almost done with my assignment. Don't forget your supper contribution."

"Good girl. Thanks for reminding me. I'm not sure what time I'll be back—maybe not until the morning if Felix takes the bait. Okay? Ring me if you have any problems. I don't care what time it is." She slipped on her strappy silver heels and straightened.

In farewell, she pressed a kiss to the girl's cheek. The sixteen-year-old hugged her back—an improvement from their first anxious months together when Gina had refused any tender touches. The genocide of their people had scarred them all. This plan had to work—they had to find a safe place amongst others of their own kind. A colony she could trust, who wouldn't report back to *that* man and place them danger.

She sighed with longing. Feline shifters might be solitary but they weren't meant to live alone.

Felix didn't feel like going to the dance at the historic woolshed but knew Saber and Emily needed privacy for a change. And in truth, he couldn't take another night of listening to their happy sex-making noise.

Man, he needed to get laid. Maybe that would shift the sense of uneasiness that had assailed him lately. Loneliness. Yeah, that was it. After seeing Saber and Emily together, he craved the same happiness his brother had found.

"Leo, you going to the woolshed dance?" Felix asked as his brother came into the kitchen.

"Nah." Leo grabbed a black leather wallet off the countertop and slid it into the back pocket of his jeans. "I'm going to Queenstown for the weekend. Why don't you come too?"

Felix fought the need to say yes and finally good conscience won. "Thanks but it's my turn to hang around and do the chores on the farm this weekend. I know Saber would do it if I asked but he deserves time with Emily."

He strolled past Leo and yanked open the fridge to pull out a beer. Returning to the seat he'd vacated, he sat, placing the can on the table in front of him.

"That's part of the reason I'm going. Since Saber mated, I feel damn edgy all the time. It's almost as if my mate is out there waiting for me. I felt it—a sort of awareness—when I was in Queenstown a few weeks ago so I'm going back to search. And if you repeat one word of this conversation to anyone, I'm going to flatten you."

Any other time Felix would have grinned and teased his brother unmercifully but Leo's words tugged a cord in him. Restless. Uneasy. Prickling skin and the urge for sex. It hammered through him relentlessly, nagging like a sore tooth.

Felix tipped back his head and drank. The beer slid down his throat, the taste of crisp hops tickling his taste buds. He swallowed and wiped the back of his hand over his mouth. "I hope you find your mate."

Leo frowned and pulled out the chair opposite Felix. He dropped onto it and peered at his brother with concern. "You too, huh?"

"Yeah."

"Who?"

Felix thought about lying but had trouble summoning the energy tonight. His life was a friggin' mess. Maybe Leo could help him make sense of the chaos. "Tomasine Brooks."

A bark of laughter erupted from Leo. "Peeping Tom, the reporter?" He studied his brother and the humor slid from his face. "Hell."

"Yeah."

"What are you going to do?"

Felix scowled even as his body sent a surge of longing thrumming to every part that would listen. He stirred, silently cursing his rising cock. He foresaw another cold shower in his future. All he had to do was think of the woman and his cock rose like a bloody warning beacon. It hadn't been like that the first time he saw her or the second. This feeling had crept up on him and sprang out last week, unexpectedly like a leaping leopard. He'd been in agony ever since.

"I've been avoiding her. It's not difficult since you can smell her coming from a block away."

"Yep, that godawful perfume she wears is better than a signal fire. Most of the shifters in town dodge her whenever they can to avoid her questions."

"Yeah, that's another reason I'm evading her. I'm sick of her questions about the black panthers. Why doesn't she give up because she's not getting information from the locals? Not since the newspaper article she wrote about the sightings near Middlemarch." Felix's gut churned at the thought of the petite dark-haired reporter. "Besides, she has career woman written all over her. I'm not going that route again."

"You sure, bro? She has a kid and a cousin who lives with her, so she can't be that involved with her career."

Felix cursed softly and chugged down more beer while he thought about his life and the way it sucked.

"Tomasine Brooks is determined to get her story. She reminds me of Alicia—the same grit and killer instinct. She might be a tiny thing, but I refuse to let her walk all over me like Alicia did. I'm not a green kid anymore."

"You can't fight the urge, not if the woman is your mate. Shit, if you're feeling half the grief I am…" Leo trailed off with an expressive shrug. "Maybe you should try a one-night stand. Perhaps it's not her."

"It's her all right." And he wished like hell it wasn't.

"But how do you know?" Leo insisted.

Felix thumped his beer can onto the tabletop and leaned back on his wooden chair. He recalled the exact moment his week had slid into the toilet.

The post office. He'd gone to pick up some stamps so he could post a couple of farm invoices and he'd bumped into her. Literally. A full shoulder-to-knee contact. He shuddered, remembering the heat that had surged straight to his cock. He'd smelled something foreign before the stench of her perfume struck him and his eyes had started to water. The need to kiss her, to rip off her clothes and take her there in the street had almost killed him.

"I almost fucked her outside the post office. That conclusive enough for you?"

Leo gaped for an instant before he found his voice. "Yeah. Okay. You might be right. Hell, outside the *post office*?"

"Scared the shit out of me. School had just let out."

"What did you do?"

"I apologized for bumping into her and hightailed it out of there. Emily bawled me out for forgetting the stamps once I arrived home. I headed straight for the shower and— Well, that's enough information. The rest is personal."

"What are you going to do?"

Before Felix could answer, the distinct sound of feminine laughter came from the far end of the house. A husky male chuckle followed.

"It's times like this that I wish our senses weren't so highly developed," Felix muttered. "The way I see it, I can stay here and think about sex because I know Saber is getting some, or I can head to the dance and think of sex there. Either way I'm screwed."

"Nah, that's your problem. You want to be screwed." Leo jumped to his feet and danced out of Felix's reach. "You want sex. You need to do it, not think about the act."

"Thank you, oh wise one," Felix snapped. "That's very helpful. Tell me what I should do."

Leo sobered. "Hell if I know."

There was silence as they pondered their collective problems. The bed started to creak down at the far end of the house.

"I'm out of here." Leo snagged a set of keys from the set of hooks just inside the kitchen door. He paused and turned around. "Maybe you should let things take their course. Go to the woolshed dance and if she's agreeable, take things from there."

Felix spewed a mouthful of beer over the flowery tablecloth, one of the many changes instigated by Emily. He leapt to his feet, grabbed a cloth from near the sink and dabbed at the marks. "You're telling me to sleep with the enemy. Man, where's your brain?"

"Same place as yours," Leo snapped. "Fuck her, dammit, and get her out of your system." He stomped from sight, leaving Felix staring after him in shock.

Leo had it as bad as he did.

A masculine groan reverberated down the far end of the house. Damn Saber and Emily. Felix considered shifting and trying to run the frustration from his system, except physical activity hadn't worked so far. He'd shifted and run out by the salt lake for hours on Tuesday, Wednesday and Thursday. Nothing he'd done had pried Tomasine Brooks from his mind. He inhaled and came to a decision—a coin toss. He'd leave his fate to the toss of the coin.

Felix rummaged around the countertop and uncovered a small bowl of change. He plucked a twenty-cent piece from the bowl and tossed it in the air.

"Heads for home," he muttered as he watched the spin of the silver coin. It came down and he snagged it in his palm and slapped it on the countertop.

"Tails for the dance." Felix stared at the face of the coin. His gut twisted and his cock chose that moment to show approval. He checked the clock on the microwave. If he hurried, he had time for a cold shower.

F elix Mitchell wasn't at the dance.

Tomasine scanned the woolshed interior, trying not to appear too obvious in her search—a bit difficult when most of the single men in Middlemarch were busy checking out her assets. She strolled past an empty wool press and ducked behind, her breasts heaving with each agitated breath. Bother, she had to calm down and quit the heavy breathing.

Grabbing attention was *not* the plan. Sure the dress molded her form, but she wasn't the only one who'd gone all out in the hope of attracting masculine attention tonight. The Mitchell brothers were an attractive proposition and since Saber Mitchell had taken a wife, the single women considered the other brothers fair game. Women from all the neighboring towns had made a point of attending the dance now that some of the bachelors seemed attainable.

The country and western band had set up on the platform reserved for the men shearing the sheep. At the far end of the shearing board, the grinder was covered to prevent injury while the shearing machines had been unbolted from their positions above the chutes. The band belted out a song about cowboys riding the range and roping steers while the attendants did an enthusiastic line dance.

Tomasine scanned the crowded shed again, searching for Felix. The wooden tables used for the shearers' smoko or meal breaks were set up against the wall as a bar with an older man and a young woman dispensing drinks. Tomasine knew their faces but not their names. She made a mental note to check on them later. Right now, she was too nervous to concentrate on questioning anyone.

What would she do if he didn't turn up?

A sigh whispered from her as she answered her own question. Wait for another night. As long as the assassins stayed away from Middlemarch, she had time.

When she caught a glimpse of a woman bearing plates of food, she followed, carrying her own contribution over to the area designated for supper. A group of older women presided over the plates, arranging the food ready for serving later in the evening and catching up on local gossip.

A flicker of envy flashed through her. These women knew their place. They fitted into the town's social hierarchy. She lacked a true home.

She fought to halt a scowl. Bernard's fault, but at least she was alive. The rest of the clan who lived on the savannah had died in the massacre, while others—Bernard and Joseph's followers—had remained safely ensconced at the new and very ostentatious palace on the outskirts of Dar-es-Salaam.

Forcing a smile, she produced her plate of pikelets. The small rounds resembling miniature hotcakes were popular at suppers such as these, or so Gina said. Tomasine wasn't the best cook or particularly experienced, but the two of them had practiced until their pikelets looked as good as they tasted. Served with strawberry jam and whipped cream, she was positive her supper offering would pass muster. Her gut churned as she realized she sought the approval of these women.

She wanted to belong—if it was safe. Which was where Felix Mitchell came in, but the man wasn't cooperative enough to attend the dance.

"Thank you, Mrs. Brooks," a tall, thin woman said.

Tomasine recognized her as one of the mothers who had a child in Sylvie's class.

"Tomasine," she corrected with a smile. Hope soared since this was a better reaction than usual. Maybe persistence was the key to acceptance. Then she overheard two of the women whispering. *Peeping Tom.*

She'd heard herself referred to in that light, and not for the first time she wished her hearing wasn't so good. And that she hadn't succumbed to anger and written the black cat story as a way of dealing with her frustration. Not that she'd intended to publish it. It was a mystery to this day and fear stalked her every time she thought about how the story had reached her editor at the paper.

More whispers followed the first, jerking her from her uneasiness. She fought to maintain a passive face, and although her smile faded, she thought she passed the test. "Please call me Tomasine."

An uncomfortable silence followed and she grimaced. Obviously the way into their affections was not via food. They were a tough sell. Circle the home wagons to protect the town. If she didn't make a breakthrough soon, it would mean another move to a different area. She must have guaranteed safety in a shapeshifter community.

Tomasine nodded at the women clustered around the supper table and moved off to grab a drink. Immediately the chatter started behind her and she huffed in frustration. Well, that had been a big success.

"Dance with me?"

Tomasine flinched as an arm slid around her waist, jostling the beaded purse she carried hitched over one shoulder. She whirled around to face the grabby male, words of anger on her lips. They died the minute she took in the man's identity.

Felix Mitchell.

His short, dark hair was rumpled while his green gaze glowed darker than normal. Tomasine stared up at him, trying her best not to gape. What was wrong with this picture? He'd sought her out voluntarily.

"Um. Okay." Great. Here was a prime opportunity to ask questions and the power of speech deserted her.

Felix took her hand in his larger one. His palm was rough and callused from working on his family farm. She suppressed a shiver of pure need with difficulty. Ever since they'd bumped into one another at the post office, she hadn't managed to get the male off her mind. Or sex. That had figured largely as well. The stubborn thought brought irritation.

All she wanted was a haven for her daughter and foster child. She didn't need a man for financial security since Bernard's insistence on her wearing a distasteful amount of jewelry at all times had worked in her favor. For once. They'd stopped at the clan village on the way back to Dar-es-Salaam after a visit to Kenya. Along with jewelry, she'd carried passports and money. No, she didn't need a man to boss her around and treat her like a straw floor mat. Tomasine had tried that scene and hadn't liked it the first time. She wasn't about to live it again.

Felix led her over to the portion of the woolshed designated as a dance floor and took her into his arms without speaking. The band finished the slow song they were playing and started another about lost love. Felix pressed her closer to his chest than necessary but it felt right.

It was the post office meeting all over again. The same swift kick in the gut, the melting feminine warmth inside and the desperate urge to rip off her clothes. His clothes. The fierce desire to press skin to skin and join emotionally as well as physically.

Tomasine surrendered to temptation and leaned in, breathing his scent. It wasn't quite the same as she remembered. There was a medicinal tang to him, as if he had taken pills or medicine. She frowned. Shapeshifters didn't require the use of human medication. Was she wrong about the Mitchell family? She discarded the thought almost immediately.

"What's the funny smell?" If he said her perfume, she might hit him. After months of using the horrid stuff, her scent glands had become immune to the chemical smell of roses and lilies. It was the best way to mask her shapeshifter identity so she was stuck with the stench.

"I had a bit of a cold. Emily suggested I use some eucalyptus. It's meant to be a good natural healer." Felix drew her back against his chest and they continued to dance to the music in silence. He guided them to the far corner where there were less people and the light seemed dimmer. Once there, he slowed his steps and they swayed rather than danced.

Now that she had him in front of her, she wanted to ask her pointed questions about black panther sightings near

19

Middlemarch and swing the conversation around to the possibility of shapeshifters, but the male distracted her. It was either that or jumping him. The brush of her breasts against his chest sent shock waves clamoring across her skin. Her heart thudded extra hard and she became aware she wasn't alone in reacting to their closeness. Felix Mitchell had an erection and it brushed against her belly with each sway of their bodies.

Satisfaction swelled in a wave, but along with the blast of happiness—because it seemed her plan to get closer to the Mitchell family might work—the realization created a chain reaction. Her breasts pulled even tighter and started to tingle. A corresponding ache sprang to life in her core and she felt an embarrassing surge of juices between her thighs.

No! This couldn't be happening. She'd thought—hoped—the incident outside the post office had been a one-off. Unfortunately not. Honesty propelled her to admit she desired him the way a female craved a mate. The shock froze her in place. She stared up at him through lowered lashes while trying to maintain her composure. Bernard was dead. The mating mark on her shoulder had started to fade after his death and had now vanished completely. She supposed it was possible to mate again, if that was what a female wanted.

Felix stopped dancing. "What's wrong?" He gazed down at her, tilting his head to the side. All she could do was stare. Such beautiful green eyes, set in his strong face. They glowed as if he found her interesting.

God, he was so sexy.

So tempting.

Distracting.

"I...nothing," she said, taking the coward's way out. Her plan was working without her doing a thing and it scared her to death. It had been so long since she'd allowed herself to think about a male in a sexual way.

But a mate?

Tomasine had thought she could allow him to use her body in exchange for information. A fair trade-off or so she'd thought. But now, walking this path, she wondered if separating her emotions from business would become an issue.

She glanced up at him and caught his quizzical expression. Blushing, she burrowed against his chest, allowing their lower bodies to rub together. She chewed her bottom lip to stem her happy sigh. Bernard had never made her feel this way, even during the heady early days of their mating.

One of the light bulbs blew above them, making the area even dimmer. The dance floor took on a new intimacy. Tomasine had no difficulty seeing so she wasn't too bothered. A rowdy group of youngsters, in their early twenties, roared in approval, and she noticed several of the couples moved closer. Felix drew her against his chest and she was left in no doubt that he was happy to see her.

Felix let out an unsteady breath when Peeping Tom—Tomasine—rubbed against the bulge in his jeans. Hell, if he wasn't damn careful, he was going to embarrass himself in public.

He stopped dancing and eased her away from his aching groin. "I'm going for a walk outside," he said, his tone abrupt. "Do you want to come?"

He waited for her to laugh and say it was too cold. Any sane woman would answer that way but instead she nodded.

Felix debated between running for the hills surrounding Middlemarch and pouncing. He was leaning toward the pounce, which wasn't the wisest move. Instead, he inhaled shallowly to avoid a lungful of her scent or the eucalyptus he'd pilfered from Emily to counteract the godawful perfume. He placed his hand at the small of her back to direct her toward the exit of the woolshed. Although he wasn't cold, he stopped to grab his coat since his higher core temperature would likely raise questions about why he wasn't feeling the chill in the air.

"You'd better grab your coat," he said.

Tomasine's brown eyes widened a fraction and he caught a hint of uncertainty. "I didn't bring a coat."

Felix felt his brows rise and then, when he caught the hint of color on her high cheekbones, understood. A solo mum, she didn't have the money to buy a coat for the winter. He softened inside and made a mental note to do something to correct the situation. No matter what her occupation, they couldn't let Tomasine and her child and young cousin want for something as simple as a coat to keep warm.

"You can share mine." Felix glanced over his shoulder to see if anyone was watching them. All clear. He helped her into his coat, encasing both her and her evening purse at once. She looked like a child playing dress up, but beneath the sheepskin-lined jacket, her body was all woman. He allowed himself a moment to touch her silky, dark brown hair. It was arranged in a complicated style on top of her head. He'd seen it loose once and wondered what the silky locks would feel like dragging across his naked chest.

A harsh swallow emerged as he struggled to control his unruly desires. Taking her hand, he ducked from the woolshed, dragging her after him. They'd given Saber such a hard time when he'd gone after Emily. From his viewpoint right now he was full of sympathy. Finding a possible mate—it wasn't as easy or as simple as the elders made out.

And here he was making it even harder for himself by consorting with the enemy.

Felix turned left by instinct, without having any destination in mind. All he wanted was to find a place where they could be in private without interruptions. They strolled past the empty sheep yards and headed for the pine trees and hayshed over at the other end of the paddock.

It had rained the previous day and there were large puddles that hadn't soaked away yet. Felix stopped walking at the edge of a puddle. "Careful, it's muddy here. Ah hell. Maybe we shouldn't be walking out here in the dark. I wasn't thinking. I'll take you back." Even though it was the last thing he wanted.

"No!"

Felix stared. "No, what?"

Tomasine pressed against his side. "I don't want to go inside."

Her face was upturned and her lips at just the right angle to kiss. When he caught sight of the tip of her tongue peeking between her lips, Felix lost the tenuous hold on his control. His head dipped to nibble at her bottom lip, to taste her luscious mouth. The startled exhale from Tomasine was something to savor. His tongue slipped between her parted lips and he took the kiss deeper.

Half of him expected a protest, a slap around the ears, but it didn't come. Instead her hands settled on his shoulders and she drew him closer, fully participating in the kiss, urging him to drink deeper. She tasted of mint and orange while her lips were smooth and soft. Delicious. Their tongues danced and flirted together until they both needed to breathe.

Slowly, Felix pulled away and stared down at her. She looked as stunned as he felt, but the closer contact settled one thing in his mind. He wanted her. Despite the fact she was the enemy, the woman responsible for bringing press attention to Middlemarch and placing them all in danger.

Was it possible this woman was his mate?

Chapter 2

Success

"Kiss me again," Tomasine murmured in a throaty voice.

No problem, but not in the middle of the paddock where anyone could witness their embrace. Tomasine Brooks might be his mate but he wanted to go slow and avoid gossip. He scooped her up in his arms and strode through the mud toward the grove of pines and the small ironclad shed used as an overflow hayshed.

"You're very strong," she whispered, relaxed and at ease in his arms.

It was like their collision all over again. The same shocked reaction to their proximity, the same desire for sex with her rocketed through him.

The enemy.

Peeping Tom.

He swallowed, trying to exert control over his racing pulse. Even so, the prickle of awareness that preceded shifting took him by surprise. Immediately, he attempted to backpedal. He thought of multiplication tables. The amount of provisional tax they needed to pay come tax time. He concentrated on everything except the woman in his arms and the surprising reaction she pulled from him. She pressed a kiss to the flesh at the V of his gray shirt.

"Aren't you wondering what I'm going to do with you?" he demanded.

"I'm pretty sure we're in agreement." Her sultry voice put a stop to his success at mentally pushing her away. He felt his canines lengthen. She might speak the truth but Felix wasn't sure they were doing the right thing.

She was a career woman searching for proof that black panthers inhabited the area around Middlemarch. He was a simple farmer who liked his life in the countryside, dealing with animals and the land. He'd done the city versus country thing and still bore the scars.

"Maybe we shouldn't go so fast." Felix set Tomasine down outside the shed and frowned down at her, trying to decide what he should do.

"Stop thinking so hard," she teased, tracing the curve of his mouth with her fingers.

The touch ignited his cock. God, he wanted to fuck her so badly he was having trouble stringing thoughts together. He snared her hand and pressed a kiss to the fragile skin at the base of her palm. His tongue swept across the network of veins there, tasting her delicate skin. Felix smelled her perfume and tasted the chemical makeup of it then caught a hint of something else that surprised him.

Shifter.

Strange. How? Then enlightenment arrived. He'd watched her hand over her plate to the ladies at the supper table. She must have touched one of the shifter females. He licked across her wrist and the scent didn't seem so strong. Hard to tell for sure with the eucalyptus blocking his scent glands.

"Ever since we collided outside the post office, I haven't been able to get you out of my mind," she said breathlessly. "I need you." A delicate blush converged in her cheeks.

He couldn't read her gaze since her lashes were lowered, her thoughts screened.

"I need you inside me."

Well, that was blunt, but since their desires had united on the subject, he could hardly complain. A shiver worked through him when she drew her hands over his shoulders. She slid her hands down his back until, finally, she cupped his butt. She squeezed his buttocks through his jeans. Not the touch he wanted but acceptable. They could progress from there.

"I...feel the same way," Felix said, stomping over a self-imposed line.

"Thank goodness," she replied, her lilting tone echoing the relief in her words. "For a moment I thought you were going to tell me to go away. Just like the rest of the people in this town."

"This had better not be about those bloody black cats," Felix snapped. Her words put the brake on his shift, jerking him firmly to human. Thank god. "If it is, I'll take you back to the dance. I don't know how many times we have to tell you the cats don't exist. Those tourists you spoke to were drunk. You should forget your story and return to Dunedin."

"It's not about the cats." Her cheeks flushed with a delicate pink even as she winced at his accusation. She brought to mind a sexy fallen angel and his distrust eased.

Tomasine stood on tiptoe and brushed a kiss across his mouth then nipped his bottom lip before backing away to stare at him in challenge. "This is about sex. I'm tired of being alone and I'm attracted to you. I thought the desire was mutual. If I'm mistaken, tell me now." Her chest rose and fell in agitation and all of a sudden one plump breast popped from beneath the straining green material of her bodice.

Felix stared at the pale globe and the coral-colored tip that drew tight as he watched. *Okay, that was it.* He was no fool. He quashed his last remaining scruples and reached out with a trembling hand to touch her breast. Her skin was soft, enticingly soft, and he bent his head and licked from base to tip, savoring the contrast of his abrasive tongue against her silky flesh.

His mate. The knowledge washed through him and he welcomed the disturbing newsflash.

Tomasine gripped his upper arms as if she feared he'd push her away. Wouldn't happen. No way. No how. She was his mate. He was positive of it now.

His frustrations were at an end, and he could settle to enjoy her. His tongue circled her nipple and a feral smile sprang to life. If she knew how desperate he was, how he'd fight to the death if he thought someone might stop him from thrusting into her body tonight. The savage notion gave him pause.

God, when he next saw Saber, he was going to ask questions. No matter how embarrassing the discussion of sex with his older brother might be, he intended to persist.

His mouth fastened over the taut peak, going for direct rather than subtle teasing. A groan slipped from her. Felix tongued the tip and realized her flesh tasted of *her* instead of the perfume. She smelled of cinnamon and vanilla—a warm feminine scent that made him eager to explore further. For an instant, he thought he caught a shifter scent again but decided it was his imagination.

"Harder," Tomasine instructed, tugging at his ears and trying to hold him in place. "Oh please, please suck me harder, dammit."

Felix grinned. For a wee bit of a thing, she was mighty bossy. After pushing his coat off her shoulders and tugging it down her arms, he massaged her breast with the fingers of one hand. Desperate to see more, he tossed the coat aside and dragged down the bodice of her dress. With little encouragement on his part, the material sagged to her waist.

Even though it was very dark, he had no trouble seeing the bounty he'd revealed. Her breasts were full and more than a handful. Beautiful, Felix thought, deciding in that moment he was a breast man. He sighed. Oh yeah. Definitely a breast man.

"I'm waiting," Tomasine said with a trace of impatience. "You do know what to do?"

A splutter of laughter escaped him, the first real humor he'd felt since the post office episode. "You besmirching my manhood?"

"Who me?"

"I don't see anyone else here." But they were still in plain view and the wind had picked up. Since he intended to strip every single item of clothing from her sexy form, they needed a sheltered place. Felix tried the door of the hayshed and was glad to find it unlocked. After scooping up his coat, he hustled her into the dark barn.

The scent of hay was warm and familiar, bringing back boyhood memories. The bales were the small rectangle shape and light enough for a single man to lift without over exertion. He left the door open a fraction so it wasn't too dark inside. He didn't want to scare her—yeah, that was the last thing he wanted.

He turned to her and grinned. "I'll have to persuade you I'm all man."

A fine tremor went through Tomasine. She didn't need persuading but she wouldn't mind proof. Talk cost nothing. She knew *that* from experience. A man had to walk the walk before she came close to believing in them.

"Show me." *And please hurry*. Her breasts were prickling something fierce and her pussy ached for a man. The urge to shift was strong but she fought it, knowing that once he entered her, the desire would leave, driven out by the feline sexual hormones that swam through her blood. At the back of her mind she wondered why the compulsion to get close to him called so strongly. It hadn't been like this before. Yes, she'd felt overwhelmed, felt desire, but it had faded. Bernard had called her defective. All it took from Felix was a look, a touch, the sensation of his sexy green gaze roving her body.

"Dammit, I intend to show you. You, madam, are impatient and bossy. Give me a break. I want to savor as well as get my rocks off. There hasn't been anyone for a while and I want to go slow. I want it to be good for both of us, to live up to the promise I felt outside the post office."

"Oh." Tomasine felt incredibly flattered since his words throbbed with honesty. It wasn't just a smooth line to garner sympathy and she liked his confident attitude. She set her beaded purse aside in a place where she'd remember to grab it on leaving. He would be so easy to love even though she couldn't allow that to happen. Not now...

Felix shifted several bales of hay with smooth efficiency, lining them up in the shape of a bed. Tomasine watched, mesmerized by the smooth pull of muscles beneath his body-fitting shirt. She couldn't wait to see him unclothed at close quarters. A glimpse caught while spying on the brothers had started her wishing for a good look. Touching... She tamped down a nervous giggle.

He grabbed his coat and smoothed it on top of the hay before turning back to her with purpose in every line of his sexy body.

"Time to get you naked."

Tomasine would rather he whipped his clothes off so she had a better view but at least they were moving ahead again instead of dallying.

"Come here," he said, his eyes glowing and a flash of golden highlights appearing.

A hint of shapeshifter on display. Tomasine reminded herself to keep her gaze down if they ended up face-to-face. It was too early for him to learn the truth. Trust must come first. She took

31

two small steps and then another two until she stood in front of him, her breasts proudly bared for his viewing pleasure.

"How does the dress come off?"

Tomasine turned to present her back to him. "There's a zipper at the back."

He stepped close, letting her feel his body heat. His warm breath wafted against her neck and seconds later, he nuzzled the tender flesh there. Tomasine let her head roll back to savor the sensation. A purr of pleasure built deep in her chest and it erupted before she could stifle it. She tensed even as he chuckled.

"Don't hide your feelings from me. I want to know the things you enjoy."

Tomasine grimaced. Ready to spill the truth and let him learn she was a shifter like him? No—not until she was sure it was safe. "I like being touched," she snapped to cover the traces of panic unfurling inside her. Giving herself to this man was a major step, one she couldn't undo. What if it was a mistake? "You have yet to do anything apart from kiss me and tug on my nipples."

"The twins would just love that snippy mouth of yours," he murmured, his amusement clear. "I'm glad I bumped into you first. They have too much charm for their own good."

"I'm not interested in your brothers." And it was true. It was Felix who made her heart beat faster even though the Mitchell brothers were very similar in appearance. Their green eyes and black hair gave them a rakish charm while their farm-tough bodies were just plain sexy. She'd almost swallowed her tongue the other day when they'd all whipped off their shirts. Tomasine would have stayed to watch the fun but picking up Sylvie from school and collecting Gina from the bus stop came first.

He turned her to face him and she saw his open suspicion. "Why me?"

It was too soon to go into particulars, and she sought refuge in mockery. "You want me to stroke your ego?"

"I want to know why you picked me."

Persistent devil. "Because I haven't been able to stop thinking about you since we ran into each other outside the post office."

His grim expression lightened at her words. "Me neither," he admitted.

"If we're finished with the discussion, can we get to business?" Yep, no doubting it. He brought out her snippiness. She was turning into a mouthy shrew. Perhaps she needed to offer an explanation to counter any disgust. "I ache."

A tiny smile played over his lips seconds before he turned her around again. Competent hands undid her zipper and the dress fell to her feet in a whoosh of fabric. "Much better." His husky voice stroked across her nerve endings and he nuzzled her neck again.

Moving along here. Tomasine turned in his arms and gave him the full frontal view. Although she was petite, Tomasine knew without conceit that men found her attractive and her curves came as a surprise. She smiled at his reaction, the fire in his eyes and sensual twist to his mouth. Petite didn't mean lacking.

"You ready to touch me now?"

"Oh yeah," he said in a reverent voice, his gaze traveling across her naked breasts. "I thought... I mean I felt your body...but the clothes..."

"They disguised my better points."

33

He grinned, teeth a pointed white flash in the dark. "Your face is nice too." He didn't give her time to protest but dipped his head and rubbed his lips over hers. Her mouth opened and he slipped his tongue inside. Felix drew her against his chest and the friction of his gray cotton shirt against her breasts shot sensation straight to her core.

Tomasine moaned under her breath, her heart drumming in a jungle beat. Without warning, he lifted her off her feet and placed her on his jacket that he'd spread over the hay. Before she could react he leaned over her, pinning her in place by holding her upper arms. A trace of panic flickered through her hard and fast until sanity prevailed. He meant her no harm. She willed herself to relax and smiled up at him in her best enticing manner.

"You are gorgeous," he whispered, his gaze running across her breasts and down to her groin. His gaze lingered on her green panties until the heat inside her roared like an enraged beast. She stirred, restlessly fighting the urges coursing through her naughty mind. Touch. Touch. *Touch*. Rip off his clothes. Take a bite of the beautiful muscled chest. That would hurry him along. "Let me remove your shoes."

Tomasine lay quietly while he slipped the silver high heels from her feet and peeled down the thigh-high stockings. Felix's caress loitered as he reached for her panties. She shivered when his blunt fingers tickled the insides of her thighs. Her breath hitched. Of course he noticed since he was watching her expression. His lips twitched and he ran his fingers along the elastic of her panty leg, dipping callused fingers beneath the band to sear her flesh.

She tilted her pelvis upward, greedy for his touch. A more intimate contact. Felix dragged his finger across the thin fabric until he reached the top band of elastic that held them in place.

Not enough.

"Touch me," she ordered.

This time he obeyed. He ran his finger across her pelvic bone and between her legs. She relaxed a fraction until a spark of sensation spiraled from her pussy, a promise of things to come. She gulped at the feelings coursing through her. *More.* God, she craved more.

"More." Tomasine swallowed as he did as she requested. He stripped off her panties with an expertise that gave her pause, leaving her naked while he still wore every single item of clothing. It made her feel vulnerable and brought back her doubts with a screaming and painful intensity. "I..." She attempted to sit up, but he stayed her with a hand to her shoulder.

"You wanted more," he said. "I'm about to give you what you want."

"Exactly?"

Felix smiled then, and Tomasine saw the hint of danger in him. The sharp white teeth. The harsh, feral expression that shouted time for business. This male wasn't one to lead around by the nose. Silly thinking she could orchestrate their meeting. Now that they were alone...heck, nothing was going to plan.

In her mind, she'd pictured fast, furtive sex—the wham, bam, thank you, ma'am, type of fling. A quick screw this time, allowing her to get a foot in the Mitchell door. Put that way, her scheme sounded cold and calculated and not her usual agenda.

She glanced at him with growing apprehension. He had the power to hurt her because somehow—in a sneak attack—he'd engaged her emotions. It was like being on a trapeze with no safety net. Dizzying. Frightening. Wonderful.

With growing apprehension she faced the inevitable. If she felt this way, it was possible he truly was her mate.

"Well, since you haven't given me specifics of what you like, my actions might not meet your specifications. But you won't have complaints." Felix pressed a quick kiss to her lips then whispered a trail of kisses down her neck. He delved into the dip of her collarbone with his tongue and nibbled her shoulder, tormenting her. Shivers of excitement took her, each breath emerging as a pant.

Bother. Why wouldn't he hurry? Tomasine tossed her head from side to side and thrust her breasts upward, trying to tempt him into greater intimacy. Her mate. How? She didn't understand even as she accepted the truth.

He chuckled and placed a kiss on the slope of one breast then he pounced, taking her by surprise. He kneaded one breast and took the nipple of the other into his mouth. This time he hustled. It was as if he'd run out of patience and his hormones were driving him as much as hers were prodding her to action.

Her mouth dried of spit as each tug of his mouth echoed in her sex. And this was just the start. He released her nipple with an audible pop. Felix lifted his head to look at her and his eyes glowed a dark green with shards of gold. His feline surfacing.

"You're beautiful. I like the way you respond. So honestly and without pretense."

Pretense. Tomasine stifled the bark of laughter that tickled for release. If he knew how much of her life was a lie. Funny, during her confident planning she had gone through with this and controlled her emotions. After all, this was for survival—her daughter and Gina—but the man had managed to slide under her barriers with ease. And that terrified her.

Her mate...

"What's wrong?" Felix smiled up at her and brushed the back of his hand over her cheek. His tender touch raised a wealth of goose bumps on her arms and legs. Raw need pooled low. *Dangerous.* The man was definitely dangerous. "What are you thinking about?"

Tomasine swallowed, wondering how to answer him. Partial honesty. "I want you but I'm frightened one or both of us will get hurt in the process."

Second thoughts. Oh yes. Big time.

Maybe it wasn't too late to flee.

"Don't you think I'm worried too? We haven't made love yet but I'm desperate for you. I have been ever since our body collision outside the post office." Felix grasped her hand in his and placed it on his groin. Even through the fabric of his jeans, Tomasine felt the heat. His erection was huge and she couldn't resist massaging him, feeling the strength of him and his shape. He growled, a feral catlike sound, and pushed her hand away.

His chest rose and fell rapidly as if he were having trouble maintaining control. "I have a hell of a lot more to lose than you."

Tomasine froze and guilt rose to nip at her conscience. Her job. How would a reporter react to his words? She already

37

knew how she, the woman, would respond and that was the problem. She opened her mouth to fire questions at him and not a word formed. She couldn't follow through. Finally, she said, "Is Middlemarch a good place to grow up in? Did you have a good childhood?"

His bark of laughter held amusement. "I have you naked, you've felt my hard-on and you want to talk about my childhood?"

Okay, she could see his point. Heck, she'd felt it as well—the connection that arced between them. "Maybe we could talk about that later. I worry about my daughter and my cousin." An understatement. She guarded them and would do anything to ensure their safety.

"Don't worry. Middlemarch is the safest place I know," he said. "How about we talk later. If I don't get inside you soon, I'm going to need to go home to change my clothes."

Her worries were instantly supplanted by lust and the need for his cock. She imagined him long and thick surging into her. Oh yes.

"Take them off," she purred, her gaze crawling across his broad chest and lower to his obvious erection. At last, she'd see the treasures below instead of relying on her imagination. Her hands darted to his buttons but he grabbed them before she could undo any.

"Your vision is good," he said.

Shoot. "I like carrots."

"An overrated vegetable."

"Take off your clothes. I dare you. If you don't get naked soon, I'm going to think you're hiding something." She was never playful like this. Not with Bernard. Not with any male. This was new...scary almost. She was out of control. Gina had warned her the plan might backfire. Wise child.

"Not yet," he said. "I want to make sure you're ready for me."

His face turned serious. Feral. Again. Tomasine shivered but it wasn't with fear. Definitely not fear.

"Part your legs for me. Let me see—" He broke off to laugh. "Can't see much in this light but I'll imagine. I want to smell. I want to feel. Taste."

"Please." Just listening to the smoky quality of his voice twisted her insides. The flare of desire in his sexy expression decided her. Slowly she splayed her legs, watching his face the entire time.

The golden glow in his eyes intensified. She heard his hoarse breathing and smelled the sharp notes of eucalyptus. Felix palmed her breasts a little roughly but it sharpened her need. He kissed her bellybutton and used his tongue to lick and tease the sensitive region. Every touch, every sigh drove her higher. She shifted her hips, eager for his more intimate touch but a little frightened as well. She hadn't had a man since...

Don't go there.

"What? What is it?" Felix asked in an urgent voice. He brushed close, the bulge at his groin kissing her outer thigh. "Your eyes are more golden than brown." Felix stroked a finger across her cheek and her breath hitched at his words.

Oops. Concentrate. Aware he was waiting for a reply she murmured, "I haven't done this for a long time."

His hand rested on her hip, his touch burning so much she wouldn't have been surprised to find a brand marking the spot.

39

"That makes this extra special." Felix moved, placing himself between her parted legs. He stared down at her for a long moment and Tomasine knew he saw her clearly, that his sight was as good as hers in the dark hayshed. Heat pooled in her cheeks but it soon dissipated, heading to regions south under his intent green gaze. Eyes a woman could fall into and lose herself.

"I have to taste you," he whispered.

Tomasine nodded, afraid to speak in case her heart jumped out her mouth. In that moment she would have agreed to almost anything, anything to have him touch her more intimately.

Felix slipped his hand beneath her bottom and lifted her to his mouth with no further preliminaries. His tongue licked the length of her cleft. The rough sensation shot her enjoyment to new highs. Oh god. No doubting he was a shifter with a talented tongue like that. It curled around her clit and dipped into her entrance on the return journey.

A groan pulled from her at the next violent spasm of pleasure. She trembled, wanting more, desperate for just a bit more. Felix lifted his head to look at her. For a long moment he stared and apprehension followed. She could hardly spray perfume there. She prayed the perfume coating the rest of her skin and the highly scented bath products she used would do the trick. Her heart pounded until he lowered his head again and used one hand to part her folds. He licked her again—a long, leisurely lick that skimmed her nerve endings and had them snapping to attention. He barely touched her swollen clitoris but tremors shook her body anyway as he feasted on her slick folds.

Tomasine squeezed her eyes shut and concentrated on the sensation, the feel of his tongue lapping at her flesh. His tongue curled, dipping into her pussy. The abrasive caress shot fire through her veins. Except it wasn't enough, not nearly enough.

"Please," she whispered.

"Please what?"

"Stroke my clit," she wailed.

With a soft laugh, he answered her plea. His tongue circled her clit, sending a shower of tingles through her sensitized body. He massaged the nub with excellent attention to detail. Back and forth. Back and forth. Back and forth.

Tomasine sucked in her breath. With just a few touches she was so close, so desperate for him to give her more.

Felix savored her taste, recognition exploding through him. She tasted of shapeshifter. He'd thought he'd captured a hint of shifter earlier and pushed the thought away as impossible. His heartbeat quickened as he lapped at her juices and teased her closer to orgasm. It hadn't taken much. He knew she hovered close because her muscles tensed, like a taut bow ready to fire. A shifter who was hiding her identity. That might answer some of the questions about her persistent queries, but it raised even more.

Tomasine whimpered at the brush of his tongue across her clit. The swollen nub vibrated beneath his tongue and she cried out again. Dammit, it was almost a purr. He curled his tongue around her clit and pressed lightly. She gasped and he smiled against her flesh. Questions later. Right now they had better things to do.

Felix applied himself to the task at hand. He squeezed her soft bottom and covered her clit with his mouth. Using his lips to tug and his tongue to brush lazily across the swollen bundle of nerves, he teased her.

She shuddered, a full body tremor seconds before she came hard with a catlike screech loud enough to hurt his ears. He continued tonguing her until the quakes in her body ceased then swept his tongue down her cleft and dipped into her pussy. He smothered a groan at her taste, her scent. His mate. He knew it with every particle and the need to claim her sucked at his control.

Felix sprang away from Tomasine and pushed to his feet, making short work of his clothes. His boots and socks were flung off and tossed aside. His shirt fluttered to the ground and his jeans and boxer shorts followed. He stopped to grab a condom from his jeans pocket and ripped the wrapping away. Seconds later his cock was sheathed and he turned back to Tomasine.

His mate.

A shifter.

Felix smiled and dropped to her side. He smoothed strands of hair from her face and felt the sudden need to experience her loose hair drifting over his body. Without asking permission, he sought the clips that fastened her hair and tugged them free. To his surprise, she lifted her head to help make it easier for him. Gradually, he worked the strands until dark brown hair with hidden streaks of blonde and red tumbled loose around her shoulders. It was beautiful even though it smelled of her horrible perfume. A means to hide her scent and her identity. Now he knew.

Felix moved closer and kissed her, reveling in the feel of soft skin against his chest. Their lips met, urgent and needy, tasting and communicating their desperation for each other. He pulled away, breathing hard, the scent of perfume and eucalyptus and underlying shifter playing havoc with his senses. He wanted to enter her from behind in the traditional way. Before he could even verbalize the need, Tomasine turned her back on him and knelt on all fours. She glanced over her shoulder and caught his surprise.

"I...you don't mind, do you?" Tomasine chewed on her bottom lip, her expression shadowed with chagrin.

Felix remained silent. She'd read his mind and his balls were so tight he was in pain. He didn't mind one bit. Felix moved behind her and widened her stance a fraction. He guided his cock to her entrance and rubbed the head in her juices. Sheer, unadulterated pleasure snaked through his body, so intense Felix gritted his teeth. The spicy tang of arousal rose to greet him, bringing raw, carnal lust.

Then a prickle started, the prickle that heralded the change to feline slid seductively across his skin. Astonished, he froze, his heart pounding with fear. He couldn't change in front of the reporter.

Even though he suspected—no, knew—she was a shifter, he hated to give away his secrets. He might want to fuck her, he might know she was his mate, but it was too early to give her full access to his life, his brothers' lives or put the other Middlemarch shifters in possible danger.

43

Sweat beaded on his forehead when the change continued, his body hair increasing. His hands starting to change to claws, despite his mental screech to stop. He froze in a panic, adrenaline whooshing through his system. *Stop. Damn it, stop.* Saber hadn't mentioned anything like this happening but then they hadn't seen much of their older brother recently to discuss that sort of thing. A faint glow emanated from his hands and he hissed in alarm, fighting the change with everything he had. Panting and gritting his teeth, despite the lengthening of his canines.

Sex. The thought popped into his mind and he acted instinctively, pushing deep into her moist flesh instead of dallying. His breath eased out on a purr. It was pure heaven feeling the slick walls of her pussy clenching him firmly. Just being inside her tight channel seemed to ease the instinct to change even though he had a desperate yearning to bite and mark her flesh.

Felix pulled out until his cock rested just inside her pussy. She waggled her butt at him, dislodging his cock. They both groaned, a sound of disappointment.

"Hurry," Tomasine said.

"Why? We have all night."

Tomasine tensed for an instant. He felt her tension as he gripped her hips to guide himself back into her pussy. A pent-up breath eased out when he pushed inside her again. Secrets. The woman held them close to her chest but now he knew they were there…

Felix plunged into her clinging heat, no longer worried about the change since the need had receded now that they were making love. He leaned over her, dominating her pliant body with his strength. Felix thrust, setting up a rhythm that pleased him, slow and steady and deep. He nuzzled her neck and couldn't resist licking the delicate skin behind her ear. The taste of shifter leapt across his taste buds. She'd missed a spot while spraying the perfume. He licked again and she purred, a low, rough sound that vibrated through him straight to his balls. She tasted of the earth, of nature and all things wild and exotic. He couldn't resist a tiny nibble and felt her pussy clamp down on his cock.

He grinned and increased the speed of his strokes. As much as she tried, she couldn't hide her identity from her mate.

He caressed her shoulders and dropped his hands to cup her breasts. He tugged a distended nipple and her channel squeezed his shaft. This woman responded to every touch. Felix repeated the move, twisting his fingers a little to add a brief shard of pain. Tomasine wailed and bucked beneath him, shuddering while he almost went cross-eyed with the heavy pulsating of her sex. She was close.

Felix swallowed his grunt because so was he. He raked his tongue across the curve of one shoulder while he fingered and tugged her breasts. He'd slowed his thrusts despite the increasingly urgent hunger gripping him. She was moist and her pussy felt like molten fire clutching his cock.

Tomasine rode the hard knife-edge of pleasure that came with each of his thrusts. He was rough but it excited her. He was nothing like Bernard.

Nothing.

She shoved away the past to concentrate on Felix and the sheer physical perfection of his body as he pounded into her. His nimble fingers taunted her, tugging at sensitive nipples until she wanted to purr with the intensity of the sensations. A rumbling purr slipped free. He thrust and swiveled at the same time.

Oh yes! Just the right place.

She balanced on the threshold of magic. The first loving had been good but this...this promised to travel far beyond the realms of good. He plunged into her again, tugged at her nipple.

Felix made a dark sound deep in his throat. It vibrated through her, the feline in her rejoicing at this joining. Frissons of excitement coalesced in one achy spot.

"Oh god," he gasped.

Exactly. He felt impossibly large inside her and filled her to perfection.

"Yes," she whispered. So good. So very, very good. His thrusts took on a measure of urgency. His teeth scraped across her upper shoulder, making her tremble anew. The mating spot. Part of her wanted him to bite down, to draw blood and release enzymes to bind them. And she definitely wanted to bite him. The need ate at her restraint.

He squeezed one nipple and she toppled from the magical peak, exploding on a white-hot tide of bliss. She gasped at the heat, the savage throb of her nerve endings even as she shattered.

A true mating...

She cried out when another series of shock waves hit her. Her pussy squeezed his shaft and he tensed with a deep, heartfelt groan that reverberated through her body. His cock jerked inside her, jetting his semen in hard blasts that dragged a satisfied

46

purr from deep in his chest. She felt it while she luxuriated in a haze of afterglow.

She smelled their combined scents, the cloying rose and lily made stronger by the heat they'd generated. Tomasine loathed the perfume, would always hate this smell, but she was stuck with it until assured of their safety.

Felix stilled and swept aside her hair to kiss her spine. His chest was damp and a little sticky as he pressed against her still in the dominant position. Tomasine sighed. She liked this male but she needed to test him before she gave her full trust.

Chapter 3

Confusion

On entering the family home the next morning, Felix found it quiet. Still early. Saber and Emily had succumbed to exhaustion. Thank god! He glanced at his watch. Seven o'clock. They'd been holed up in their bedroom since yesterday afternoon. It was time they came out for air. He stalked along the passage of the old homestead, the wooden floors creaking beneath each determined step.

Felix pounded on the door, thinking of the expression on Tomasine's face at their parting. A timid smile. After much thought, he decided to talk to his family and formulate a plan before he spoke of her feline genes, before he let Tomasine know her secret was out.

They'd spent most of the night in the hayshed—he didn't think he'd be able to enter one again without getting a hard-on and imagining sex. At dawn, they'd walked hand in hand across the hill and watched the approach of the day. Felix had never felt so comfortable with a woman but the mystery was killing him.

"Dammit, wake up!" He knocked, impatience filling each thump.

"Go away," Saber snarled, albeit a muffled growl.

Busy. Too bad. Felix applied his fist to the door again.

"Unless the sky is falling come back in two hours," a feminine voice ordered. His sister-in-law Emily.

"The damn sky is falling," Felix snapped. "Get decent and come out." He heard a whispered conversation between his brother and his mate. "I'll make coffee," he said, retreating once rustling came from within the bedroom.

Felix stopped by his bedroom and changed into work clothes. A red bruise stood out on his biceps and he smiled, pleased at the souvenir of his night spent with Tomasine. Felix pulled on jeans and shrugged into a faded T-shirt, then headed for the kitchen. His mind still on his night with Tomasine, he dumped the old coffee filter in the rubbish and topped the reservoir with fresh, cold water. After opening the fridge and peering at the contents, he grabbed a loaf of bread, some butter, marmalade and jam and put them on the granite countertop. By the time Saber and Emily made an appearance, the scent of coffee spiced the air.

Felix poured three mugs and placed them on the table. Without being asked, he grabbed the jar of Vegemite from the pantry, set it next to Emily's plate and sat to wait.

Saber took a sip of his coffee and glared at him. "We weren't ready to get out of bed. What the hell is so all-fired important that you needed to interrupt us?"

"Tomasine Brooks is a shifter."

Saber stiffened, his stare incredulous, then he gave a bark of laughter.

"Peeping Tom?" Emily demanded as she grabbed her glasses off the counter and pushed them into place. "She's the reporter."

Felix nodded.

"How do you know?"

"Her scent," Felix said.

"How could you smell anything other than the perfume she wears?" Saber took another sip of coffee. "She reeks of the stuff. Every respectable shifter in Middlemarch can smell her coming from a kilometer away."

"Even I can smell her," Emily said. "And I'm plain, ordinary human."

Saber drew her close and pressed a kiss on her lips. "Nothing ordinary about you, kitten."

They shared a grin that a few days ago would have driven Felix from the house. But now after spending the night with Tomasine, his heart clamored for the same intimacy with his mate.

"I think she's a shifter like us," he reiterated.

"Did you question her?" Saber asked.

Emily reached for a piece of toast and placed it on the plate he'd set out for her. She added butter then reached for the Vegemite. Seconds later, she slathered the thick black yeast spread over her toast. Felix winced. He'd never liked the stuff.

"Stop staring at my mate and answer," Saber snapped.

"He stares like that every morning," Emily said, unconcerned. "It's the Vegemite. You should be used to it."

"I wanted to talk to you first." Felix ripped his gaze off Emily as she lifted a triangle of toast to her lips. "There must be a reason she's hiding her true identity. A reason she's here in Middlemarch."

"Then why did she write a story about sightings of black cats?" Emily asked.

Felix heard a vehicle pull up outside the house. "Sounds like Leo. He told me he intended to spend the weekend in Queenstown."

His younger brother stalked into the kitchen, a scowl entrenched on his face. Felix took that to mean he hadn't located his mate. A surge of sympathy filled him. He knew what it was like—the yearning, the desperate need. Shit, facing up to the fact a mate roamed out there was bad enough, but not being able to find them when every sense screamed their presence was worse. Felix stood to grab another mug and poured a coffee. He handed it to Leo and returned to his seat.

They all stared at each other in silence for a while. His older brother, Saber, appeared full of satisfaction while Leo looked as if he might punch the next person who dared speak to him. Felix sipped his coffee, his thoughts slipping to Tomasine. He'd never enjoyed secrets.

"You fucked her."

Felix's head jerked up to meet Leo's gaze. Although his brother radiated anger, his dark brows drawn together, Felix caught a flicker of envy.

"Don't mind me," Emily said tartly. "I might be smaller than you but I'm sure Saber will help me hold you down so I can wash your mouth out with soap."

Felix snorted at the picture her words presented while his older brother grinned.

"Anything for you, kitten." Saber narrowed his gaze on Leo. "Mind your mouth around Emily."

"Sorry." Leo's shoulders slumped in patent unhappiness and Felix empathized with him.

"We need to talk about sex." Felix figured sex was as good a topic as any to start this discussion.

Emily's eyes rounded and mouth popped open to reveal vegemite-coated teeth. "Oh you poor boy. Don't you know how?"

"Of course I know how." To Felix's annoyance heat gathered in his cheeks. Dammit, having a female around the place put a different complexion on their round-table chats. They had to watch what they said and now it seemed censorship ruled. "Is this the thanks I get for making you toast?"

Saber smoothed his hand over the untidy fall of his wife's hair. "Shush. This isn't the time for teasing." He directed his gaze to Felix and then to Leo. "I had no knowledge of this until I found Emily. Uncle Herbert never mentioned a thing but when you find your mate, you might have an overwhelming need to shift. Hell, the first time with Emily I went through a partial change. I meant to warn you all but we haven't been together in the same place and I've been busy."

"As you should be," Emily said with approval.

"It's bloody difficult to concentrate and you might have the urge to bite and mark your mate straightaway. Control was easier once we'd had sex a few times."

"Almost as if the sex soothes the feline genes," Felix said thoughtfully. "What about now?"

Emily gave an exclamation of horror and slapped her hand over Saber's mouth. "You are not talking about our sex life."

"We hear it enough," Leo grumbled.

Felix was glad to see Leo's lighter mood. "Might pay to tell the twins next time they ring. It gave me a hell of a fright."

"Me too," Saber said dryly.

"So that's why you liked sex from the rear," Emily blurted.

"Hey, sis." Felix reached over and tugged a lock of her hair, real affection for his sister-in-law curving his lips. "Too much information."

Emily gave a mortified moan. "Perhaps this is a good time to talk about Peeping Tom. If she's a shifter, will her daughter be one too?"

Felix exchanged a glance with Leo then Saber, surprise and astonishment rebounding between him and his brothers.

Saber shook his head and said what they were all thinking. "A female shifter child. That's pretty unusual. Most of them are boys."

"Doesn't she have a cousin?" Emily asked. "Could she be a shifter as well?"

Leo whistled. "Well, hell. Three female shifters. Do you think it's possible? They all smell of the perfume. Do you think that's why?"

"What are we going to do? How do we discover the truth? And how did she know where to find us?" Felix knew what he wanted to do, and that was hunt the female down and take her somewhere private. He wanted to confront her and demand she tell him the truth. But most of all, he wanted to fix whatever had

53

driven her to withhold her identity from her kind. He frowned as he pondered the possibilities. It had to be something big.

Saber grabbed a piece of toast. "I'll talk to the elders this morning. Do you know where she comes from? As far as I know, there are no other permanent shifter communities in New Zealand."

Emily drained her coffee and stood to grab the pot. She topped up everyone's mug before returning the empty carafe to the coffeemaker and flicking off the power switch. "I believe she comes from Australia but her accent is more English. Not that I've spoken with her in any detail." She returned to her seat. "Do the shifter colonies in other countries have contact with each other?"

Leo leaned back in his chair until the front legs left the ground. "Felix, do you know? I presume you guys did talk a little last night."

Felix decided he could suffer teasing if it stopped Leo from dwelling on his mystery mate. "We talked."

"And what did you learn?" Emily asked.

"Nothing I care to share," Felix said, thinking about the way it felt squeezed deep inside her pussy, the way she purred when he touched her. Her scent. He imagined her natural aroma and a satisfied purr rattled his throat. He couldn't wait to wallow in her true scent. Perhaps they could try making love in the shower. His cock tightened in a lustful stab against his fly. A shower would be the first of many places he'd make love to her...

"Mind out of the gutter." Emily jabbed him in the ribs. "We need a plan not daydreams. And we need to learn why she wrote that story."

Felix grabbed a piece of toast. It was cold, but he buttered it and spread raspberry jam over it anyway. While Saber was discussing Tomasine with the elders, maybe he'd do a little snooping of his own.

Tomasine crept into Sylvie's bedroom to check on her daughter. Although she trusted Gina implicitly—they'd been through a lot during the last two years and she knew Gina would protect Sylvie with everything she had—she always felt better once she reassured herself of Sylvie's safety. As normal, only the top of her daughter's head showed above the covers, her long black hair cascading across the white pillow. Tomasine took a deep breath before creeping from the room. She passed her discarded shoes and bag in the hall, humming under her breath.

After scanning the newspaper she'd picked up on the way home, watching the latest of the news headlines on the television to check for any clue as to Joseph's activities and drinking several cups of coffee, Tomasine headed for the shower.

As she ambled toward the bathroom, her mind drifted to Felix and the warmth of his body draped over hers, the thrust of his cock and the intense pleasure that still simmered through her mind.

Inside the compact bathroom, Tomasine slipped off her stockings and reached behind her back to undo her zipper. One careless shrug was all it took for the dress to slide down her body. She pushed aside the plastic shower curtain to flick the shower control and wriggled out of her panties. The pipes clacked and groaned but gradually the water ran warm enough for her to enter the shower. Water streamed over her head and down her face and chest. She reached for the shampoo and smiled.

Her muscles ached in a pleasant way, and she bore sore spots on her shoulders where Felix had nipped her during his climax. Not enough to break the skin but enough to drive her pleasure higher. Her pussy moistened at the thought.

Sex with Bernard had never been like that—it had been hard and brutal and he'd taken her whenever and wherever he'd desired. No matter who was present. She had grown to hate her husband. If he hadn't died, betrayed by his cousin Joseph when he'd tricked them both into visiting the clan members on the savannah, she might have succumbed to her growing rage and done the job herself.

Tomasine washed her hair, rubbed soap over body and rinsed, aware the girls would wake soon. Her plan to question Felix had failed because of his successful distraction. *And how*. A scowl formed as she flipped the water off and reached for a towel off the chrome rack attached to the wall. She never allowed herself to become distracted in that way.

A knock sounded on the bathroom door. "Tom, hurry and get dressed. You have a visitor." The urgency in Gina's voice galvanized her to action. Her heart pounded as she wrapped the skimpy towel around her body and opened the door to peer from the bathroom. The coast was clear. She scampered down the short passage just as the front door opened. Felix stepped inside followed by Leo. They stooped to remove their shoes then straightened to watch her in silent contemplation. Their close attention brought apprehension.

"Don't you wait until you're asked to enter?" Tomasine snapped.

"Gina told us to come inside," Leo said in amusement. "She's making coffee."

Gina would because she had a crush on the man and knew Tomasine was interested in Felix. Tomasine pushed back the sudden fear she felt at having two strangers in her house. After the previous evening, she could place Felix in the safe category. He'd had ample opportunity to kill her yet she remained alive to tell the tale. A risk, but she hadn't been getting anywhere with the Middlemarch shifters, not in her reporter guise.

"She didn't tell you to gawk at Tomasine's legs," Felix said, shunting his brother toward the room they used as a combined living and dining room. The kitchen was off these rooms. She heard the clank of the taps and pipes when Gina ran the water, probably to make the proffered coffee.

"Aw, you spoil all my fun," Leo said, but he stepped out of sight and not long after Tomasine heard him talking to Gina. She heard an answering giggle and smiled. That was what she wanted for both girls—a slice of normality. Innocent flirtation and teenage crushes. Heck, even the odd tantrum or two would work.

"Morning, sweetheart." Felix's green gaze gleamed as he closed the distance between them.

Alarm struck. Fresh from the shower, it was too late to spray perfume. She backed up, but Felix was too quick for her. With two strides, he reached her and yanked her into his arms. His lips slammed down on hers in a rough and possessive kiss.

He clasped her to his chest, plundering her mouth, his fingers tunneling into her wet hair.

A moan formed in her throat as jolts of pleasurable excitement made a sneaky attack on her commonsense. Her grasp of the towel loosened as she wrapped her arms around his neck in a tight embrace.

Her mind and body recalled her enjoyment of the previous evening and that increased the sensations coursing through her now. Moisture pooled at the juncture of her thighs as he pushed past her control with his wandering hands and talented mouth. The man annihilated her willpower, yet she couldn't regret the pleasure that roared through her in exchange.

His large hands cupped and kneaded her bottom and she felt the thrust of his cock against her stomach. His scent, masculine with a hint of soap, drifted to her receptors. More. More. *More.* She craved a soft bed with Felix thrusting between her legs.

"Mama!" The terrified scream of horror ripped through her sexual fantasies.

Tomasine struggled for freedom. Felix spun around, keeping her behind him while footsteps thundered across the wooden floor of the old farmhouse. Gina appeared in the hall, followed by Leo.

"What is it?" Gina crouched low, her gaze fierce as she scanned the hall.

"Mama!" Sylvie sounded panicked and terrified.

With unsteady hands, Tomasine reached for her towel and covered her nakedness. She stepped from behind Felix but Gina beat her to Sylvie. Her daughter wore her favorite pink dress and green frog gumboots with protruding yellow eyes on her feet.

Her midnight-black hair needed a good brush while her wide brown eyes blazed with terror. Her rosebud mouth trembled, underlining her confusion at finding big men inside the house.

"Don't be scared, Sylvie. These are Tom's friends. I was making them a cup of coffee. Would you like to help?" Gina asked, hugging the little girl. "They're big but they're not very scary."

An immediate protest rose to Tomasine's lips but a warning glance from Gina tamped it down. Gina was right. She'd set the wheels in motion last night. They had to follow through. Hopefully through Felix she could learn more about the shifters and gain the insider knowledge she sought. And the big one, were they in contact with the shifter clans in Africa?

"Mama?" Still Sylvie sought reassurance and it made Tomasine sad. Angry. Fear shouldn't fill a child's life.

"It's all right, Sylvie." Tomasine tightened her grip on her towel and went to her daughter. She squatted so she was at her daughter's height and kissed her button nose, knowing it would make Sylvie giggle. "You go with Gina while Mama gets dressed."

"I dressed myself."

"Good girl. So you did." Her daughter had made free with a perfume spray. The wretched stuff made Tomasine's eyes tear but she smiled encouragement anyway. "Off you go with Gina."

"I sprayed myself."

Tomasine closed her eyes, wondering what Felix and his brother thought. "You're a good girl, Sylvie. I'm very proud of you."

59

Sylvie nodded, threw her arms around Tomasine's neck and squeezed, letting go just as quickly. She ran to Gina, chattering at a rapid pace as was her habit. Gina ushered Sylvie and Leo to the kitchen, leaving Tomasine alone with Felix.

Tomasine hesitated, not sure she wanted to witness his expression. She straightened as his hands curled around her shoulders.

"I'd better get dressed."

"I'll help," Felix said.

Tomasine snorted. "I doubt your help would be productive."

"If you mean I'd want to kiss every inch of your skin before you hid it with cloth, then you could be right," he conceded. "Your daughter is pretty."

"Thank you." She steeled herself, waiting for the inevitable questions.

"Where is Sylvie's father?"

Tomasine bit the inside of her lip hard and allowed sorrow to form on her face. "He died in an accident over two years ago." Clan infighting and genocide fitted the accident category.

"I'm sorry." Felix stepped closer and she felt the heat coming off him. She wondered what it would be like to run with a beloved mate, to run with family again in feline form. Leaping in trees and racing across the savannah with not a care in the world. The seductive thoughts appeared when she hadn't allowed herself to think of them for years, of how she missed socializing with her own kind and how much she craved the shift to cat. She hadn't wanted to risk a change while things remained so uncertain.

Tomasine swallowed to rid her throat of the lump of emotion that threatened to close her airways. "I'd better hurry. Really." She sought refuge in humor. "I'm a big girl now. I can dress by myself."

Felix nuzzled behind her ear and she felt his tongue lick across the sensitive skin. Immediately her body jumped to high alert.

Wanting him. *Again*.

"I'll wait for you in the kitchen with the others."

"Okay." She turned away, a trifle breathless and definitely full of anticipation.

"Tomasine."

"Yes?" She turned with a smile.

"Please don't put on any perfume when you're dressing. I don't like it."

Chapter 4

Puzzling Woman

F elix turned away but not before he caught the fleeting terror in her expression. He wanted to tell her everything would be all right, that he'd never hurt her. Tell her she could trust his family. Him.

Instead, he headed for the laughter and giggles, determined more than ever to learn the truth about Tomasine Brooks. He smirked at the picture he saw on entering the lounge.

Leo perched on a chair with Tomasine's daughter sitting on his lap. One of his hands curled around a coffee mug while the other circled the child's waist to stop her falling. He looked so uncomfortable Felix wanted to chuckle aloud. No doubt the perfume was knocking him out too. That wouldn't help matters.

"Ah, Felix." Leo's hearty tone underlined his uncertainty with the child. But at least he'd lost his earlier depression. "I'm going to take the girls to breakfast at Storm in a Teacup. Gina suggested it to give you guys some privacy."

His brother appeared appalled but Gina danced in excitement. She fluttered her lashes at Leo and a flush covered her chubby olive complexion. His brother had made another conquest. That would teach him for being the pretty one.

"As long as Tomasine agrees." Felix glanced around the compact rooms. From where he stood next to the dining room table, he could view the entire lounge plus the tiny kitchen. Although everything was clean, the chairs and other furniture spoke of long use and age, as if Tomasine had purchased them secondhand or inherited them from the previous tenant. The exception to this was the television set. He'd noticed the satellite antennae on the roof before he'd entered—a necessary item in Middlemarch since radio and television reception was poor.

"Mama, we're going to Storm in a Teacup," Sylvie said, naming the local café when Tomasine appeared dressed in jeans and a pale mauve T-shirt.

"Oh no. I don't think so." Tomasine cast a nervous glance in his direction and guilt surfaced. He hadn't meant to frighten her with the perfume comment but they needed to talk. He needed to learn the truth in order to protect her and her family.

"I promised the girls," Leo said. "They'll be quite safe with me."

Felix wouldn't have caught the look of panic if he hadn't been watching Tomasine so carefully. It was a deep-seated fear and anguish that caught his gut and tweaked his curiosity. What would put that sort of fear into a woman's face? She'd told him her husband was dead but maybe that was a lie. A runaway wife? His hands curled to fists at the idea of another man before blowing out a calming breath. There was no mating mark on her upper shoulder.

No, he was her destined mate and the sooner she acknowledged the fact the better.

"Please let us go, Tom," Gina said. "It will be fun."

Tomasine and Gina seemed to exchange a conversation without words. Eventually, Tomasine gave a stiff nod although appeared unhappy with the development.

"Our sister-in-law Emily works there," Felix said, trying to allay her uneasiness at letting the girls out of her sight. He knew they both attended school. She'd relaxed enough to have them out of her sight for several hours of the day. "I bet Emily will rustle up some special treats for little girls."

"Goodie." Sylvie clapped her hands and jumped off Leo's knee, almost falling. Leo caught her before she came to harm but one frog-green gumboot dropped to the floor.

"Your hair needs brushing." Tomasine held out her hand to her daughter. The child pouted but eventually trotted off to have her hair tidied, leaving Felix free to observe the teenager.

Gina, Tomasine had called her. She bore little resemblance to Tomasine or the child. Gina fell on the chubby side with a mop of short blonde curls and beautiful sparkling hazel eyes. She needed a brush as well. She wore jeans and a tight-fitting black T-shirt and looked much like the other teenagers he'd seen around Middlemarch. Was she shifter too?

Hard to tell with the stench of the perfume still filling the air.

Felix grinned. Difficult to believe, but once they sorted this mess out and he and Tomasine were together, he'd be a stepfather. The thought blew his mind. A family. Perhaps not so good for a sex life but he had brothers he could utilize if he required privacy. Saber and Emily came to mind. Payback for the mental suffering he'd had to go through while listening to them. Yeah, they'd definitely top the babysitting list.

Leo stood and closed the distance between them. "Make use of the time, bro. You're going to owe me big time."

"It will give you a chance to become acquainted with your new nieces," Felix shot back in a low undertone.

"You're certain of your ground."

Felix met his brother's gaze. "She's my mate. I don't want another woman."

Footsteps behind him made Felix turn. Tomasine had changed Sylvie's clothes and the child was dressed in trousers and a warm sweatshirt with runners on her feet. Her dark hair was restrained in a braid and she looked as cute as the cupcakes Emily made for the café. His child, he thought in awe. Protectiveness flooded him. Whatever Tomasine feared, they would face it together.

"Ready to go?" Leo asked.

"Are we going to walk?" Gina asked.

"No, I'll take the ute," Leo said, referring to the farm utility pickup they'd driven over to Tomasine's house. "It's too cold to walk." He winked at Felix. "I'll be a couple of hours, I reckon. Hell, I must be mad."

Felix stepped to Tomasine's side and slipped an arm around her waist. Her face appeared pale and worried, and he hated knowing he was hurting her. But she wasn't wearing perfume. He breathed in her scent and shifted aside her damp hair to nuzzle her neck. He fought the growing desire to bite.

"They'll be fine with Leo," he reassured her. "Emily is at the café baking cakes. If I know her, she'll set the girls to work in the kitchen. They'll have fun."

Tomasine sniffed. "It's hard enough letting them go to school." She turned to face him and stared, lifting her chin even as her fists clenched. "You know."

Felix nodded. "Why all the pretense, sweetheart? You could have told us. You didn't need to pester us with questions or seduce me. Although, I'm glad you did. Seduce me, that is." As he'd planned, his words drew a snort and lightened the worry lines on her forehead.

"You put the moves on me, mister. It wasn't all one-sided."

"No, which is why you're going to give me the quick version of the truth and let me take you to bed while we have the opportunity."

Tomasine swallowed. "Can't we go to bed right now?"

Cancel the talk. He speared her a look, saw her swallow. Tomasine was having a hard time trusting him, and it irked him. The sex could wait. They'd have plenty of chances. This week. Next week and all their tomorrows. "No, we need to talk."

The silence lengthened, became strained.

Felix decided to ask questions to prod her along. "Are Sylvie and Gina shifters too?"

"Yes. Black leopard."

"The same as us." Felix tugged her hand and led her over to a faded green couch. He pushed her down and took the seat beside her. He purposely crowded her, making sure as much of their bodies touched as possible. From shoulder to knee, he pressed against her side, the contact easing his irritation.

His mate.

Felix hadn't believed he'd find a mate in Middlemarch.

A shifter mate. He'd resigned himself to remaining single since he refused to live in the city with Alicia or attempt to lure a city girl into the country life, and then Tomasine had waltzed onto the scene. Life was good.

"Where did you come from?"

Tomasine plucked at a piece of fluff on her jeans-clad knee. "I can't tell you."

"Why?" What was wrong with the female? He was trying to help.

"It's dangerous." Tomasine glanced up, saw his displeasure and focused on her hands. "It's not safe. All I wanted was a secure place to put down roots and raise Sylvie and Gina."

"You're safe here."

She shrugged. "Maybe."

"You are safe in Middlemarch. Is that why you were asking so many questions?"

Tomasine gulped. "Yes."

"But I don't understand why you wrote the story about the black panther sightings if all you wanted was a safe place to live. You drew attention to us."

"I know," she whispered. "No one would talk to me. I became frustrated with my lack of progress. Haven't you ever done that? Acted unwisely and regretted it afterward. I'd take the story back if I could. In fact, I didn't intend to run the cat story but there was a mix-up and it was published instead of the one I'd written about the history of Middlemarch."

SHELLEY MUNRO

"It didn't occur to you it's now unsafe for the shifters who live here?" *Of all the stupid reasons.* Felix waffled between putting her over his knee to smack sense into her and holding her tight to reassure her of their safety. Maybe he could work both into the equation. His cock jerked at the thought and he stored the idea for later consideration.

"I'm sorry." Tomasine pinched the bridge of her nose and squeezed her eyes shut. It made her appear younger. Vulnerable. She was so tiny—petite—yet physically she'd taken him easily. His mind went with the new direction and lurched straight to sex. He imagined her lips wrapped around his cock and bit back a groan. *Focus, dammit.*

"If you won't tell me where you're from, at least tell me what danger we might face."

Tomasine swallowed, sending him a quick glance before concentrating on her clenched hands. "Assassins."

"Assassins?" Felix wanted to laugh because the idea was so outlandish. The idea of killers wandering New Zealand, let alone a small town like Middlemarch. Ludicrous. He expected her to grin and tell him she was joking but held back his response on seeing the flash of horror—memories—flickering across her expressive face. Okay, so she perceived the threat as real. "Apart from the ball, the woolshed dances and the agricultural fair, we don't have a lot of strangers coming through Middlemarch."

At least they hadn't until the feline council started arranging their events. A recent development.

"Tourists arrive on the train so they can see the gorge and to ride or walk the old rail track," she countered.

"Well, yes, but it would be easy to spot an assassin amongst a group of tourists."

Tomasine bounded to her feet. "You think?" Her breasts rose and fell in agitation. "Assassins come in all shapes and sizes. You don't know until you have a gun aimed at you or someone you love. You don't know until you see their dead eyes, the icy determination to collect their fee."

Felix drew a sharp breath. The dread in her voice told him this was a real threat to her, and the idea of his mate living in terror set his gut roiling. He cast his mind back, trying to think of the shifter colonies throughout the world. Cats were secretive creatures. The colonies tended to keep to themselves rather than socialize as the canine groups did.

He stood and pulled her into his arms despite the stiffness of her muscles. Gradually she softened except for the irregular tremors in her limbs. His arms wrapped around her, trying to communicate by touch he'd keep her safe.

Finally, the shuddering ceased and Tomasine glanced up at him, her expression wary.

Felix pressed a slow kiss to her lips. "I promise," he said. "You're safe with me. Nothing will happen to you in Middlemarch."

Tomasine ached to believe him. She did, but the need for survival ran deep. It had become second nature to hide in the shadows and trust no one. However, it was true she hadn't seen any assassins since leaving Spain. They'd been lucky to escape. She still wondered about the woman who'd appeared without warning and taken out the assassin. The dark-haired woman had disappeared before Tomasine could thank her. Since then she'd moved frequently, changing her name to Tomasine Brooks, acquiring false identities and passports in Europe, never staying in one place longer than a few weeks, distancing herself from Africa.

New Zealand was about as far from Africa as she could get. Maybe Felix was right and she should loosen up a little. She hadn't sensed danger from the Middlemarch shifters. In truth, she hadn't sensed any menace in New Zealand but her wariness and her need to keep glancing over her shoulder continued.

"I let the girls go out with your brother, didn't I?"

Felix scoffed. "The café is ten minutes from here in the middle of the town. Emily works there and you know where Leo lives."

"He could be a sleeper for the assassins." Tomasine froze even as she verbalized the idea. *It wasn't safe. Nowhere was safe from that monster.*

"All Leo is interested in is finding his mate. He's as attached to the farm as Saber and I are, a farmer born and bred. Leo is no assassin. He's never left New Zealand."

Tomasine nodded. As a rule, shifters disliked airplanes and flying, which was part of the reason she'd forced herself to board a plane again and again. Not her favorite activity but she'd managed and would do it again if necessary. Tomasine already had a contingency plan at the ready.

Plan. *Stay alive.*

Felix swept his hand through her hair, rubbing her scalp in a gentle massage. A purr of pleasure slid from her, and it was good no longer needing to hide her feline. She tipped her head back, giving him better access. He tugged on her hair and used his thumbs to make small circles at her temples. Gradually, he moved toward the crown of her head.

Tomasine moaned deep in her throat. "That feels so good."

"Good enough to move to the bedroom?" He scooped her off her feet and they were in the passage leading to the bedrooms before she could reply. "Which door, sweetheart?"

"The one right at the end." Although the house was small, it had three bedrooms, a luxury since the three of them had stayed in places where they'd slept crammed in one room. It was good for Sylvie to have her area and a little independence, even though it scared Tomasine to death. During the first weeks they'd lived here she'd checked on Sylvie and Gina during the night to reassure herself. More than once, foregoing sleep to ease her mind.

Felix strode down the passage and opened the door to her bedroom with one hand. She savored the play of muscles as he held her easily, navigating the pair of shoes she'd tossed on the blue floral mat covering the plain wooden floorboards. He placed her on the double bed and followed her down onto the plain navy-blue quilt. It bore remnants of the perfume he'd asked her not to wear and she had to agree the stuff honked. It would be good to leave the house without wearing it even though she didn't notice it as much now.

"I like your hair, the color. In some lights it looks as if you have streaks of sunset painted through the curls."

"It will smell better now that it's washed." Tomasine certainly enjoyed having sweet-smelling hair again.

Felix kissed the corner of her mouth and the tip of her nose. He sucked on her bottom lip and threaded his hands through her damp hair. Each kiss made her heart thump louder, her anticipation rise.

"We can shower together next time, but right now I want ordinary lovemaking in a bed." Felix punctuated his words with another kiss on the corner of her mouth. His whiskers rasped across her delicate skin, eliciting a tremor of delight.

She imagined the same sensation on her inner thighs and bit down on her lower lip to stop a mortifying groan.

"Simple stuff with no kink, just my body sliding into yours. Face-to-face in the missionary position."

Tomasine shivered, her breathing ragged with longing but also a touch of caution. "What sort of kink?"

His dark brows rose in a teasing manner and a tiny smile played around his sensual lips. "Why is it you zeroed in on that particular part of the conversation?"

How could she explain her sex life had consisted of degradation and embarrassment? She'd never known what Bernard would do next, what extraordinary lengths he would go to in order to climax. He'd blamed her. "My husband was into...ah, extreme stuff. It wasn't pretty or enjoyable."

Felix sat up and took her hands in his. "I would never do anything to hurt you. When we're together, if anything bothers you or makes you feel uncomfortable, all you need to do is tell me to stop." He kissed the tender skin on her inner wrist, honesty blazing from him. "But we can still explore our sexuality together. We'll have lots of fun."

"Yes," Tomasine breathed.

"Stand for me. I'd like to undress you. You looked great in the towel. Easy access. Stunning view."

"But your brother was staring at my legs."

Felix scowled. "He's male, but he won't look in future. I hope his mate turns up soon."

"His mate?"

Felix's gaze narrowed in a sign of impatience. "I don't want to talk about Leo. We don't have much time. We should make the most of it."

Tomasine stood, her belly quivering with sudden nerves. She managed a wobbly smile, and Felix responded, his face losing its fierceness as soon as his lips slanted up in a grin.

"Remember, all you need to do is tell me to stop and I will."

Somehow, Tomasine didn't think that would happen—her requesting him to halt. Her imagination danced ahead, and she visualized the slow slide of their bodies, the sound of flesh slapping flesh. The sensation of his mouth sliding across her skin and the push of his shaft into her pussy.

Her breathing grew unsteady as she studied him, his dark good looks, glittering green eyes and wind-rustled hair. He wasn't as pretty as his brother Leo. The angles of his face were harsh and sometimes stern, but she'd witnessed the kindness in him, experienced it too.

His gaze suggested intense interest. Last week he'd avoided her, as had the rest of the Middlemarch residents. A primitive throb pumped through her veins while she studied him, desire sinking to her sex.

He wanted *her*—Tomasine Brooks.

A fine tremor took her as he reached for her.

First, he cupped her face with his hands. He kissed her eyelids and her cheeks, slowly working his way to her mouth. Some of

73

his kisses were soft, like the flit of a butterfly, while others were slower, lingering and made her pulse dance to a crazy beat.

Tomasine pursed her lips ready for his kiss but he chuckled and bypassed her mouth. He nibbled her chin, then moved lower to kiss her neck. A sigh whispered from her. She was sure he'd remedy the neglect soon. Felix sucked on the side of her neck and the sensation flashed through her, frisking pleasure points on the way. She shifted her weight, the move abrading her nipples against the cups of her cotton bra.

She wished he'd hurry.

Almost as if he could read her impatience, he reached for the hem of her T-shirt and drew it upward. Their gazes met and held. Tomasine's heart seemed to stop under his intense regard. The tips of her breasts tingled and she swallowed as a raft of sudden nerves struck. *Bang. Bang. Bang.* They pounded away at her insecurities.

Was she doing the right thing?

Normally she followed her instincts. They were shouting—no, screaming—at her to grab this man, to trust him because he was her future. But her mind argued the point.

"Stop frowning." Felix's warm breath tickled her ear and set off a series of aftershocks. He tugged her T-shirt up higher to bare her stomach and pressed a butterfly kiss to the tender skin below her breasts. His thumb skated against the side of one breast and she waited anxiously for more.

She gripped the duvet cover, forcing herself to accept each of his seductive caresses even though uneasiness assailed her because the T-shirt now covered her face. Wanting someone led to vulnerability. Tension seized her muscles, and she started to protest, but he whipped the T-shirt over her head, granting her sight again to witness his sexy smile, his sparkling eyes and a cute dimple she hadn't noticed before. Unbidden, she reached out, her finger teasing the tiny hollow to the left of his mouth.

A growl vibrated through his chest. "Your touch distracts me. New rules. I want you to grip the wooden rails on the headboard."

She narrowed her gaze, lifted her chin. "I like the sound of you doing all the work but I want to touch too."

"Next time," Felix promised. "You have a turn next time."

Chocolate. An experiment with chocolate body paint. That would work for starters and maybe she could think up something else that would push him from his smugness. *Push.* No, she'd think of something special to blast him from complacency.

"Sounds good to me." Tomasine couldn't help the smug chirpiness in her voice as she gripped two of the wooden slats on the headboard and held tight.

Felix leaned over her, his lips halting a fraction from hers. If she pursed her lips, their mouths would touch. "What are you thinking?" Both suspicion and amusement filled his words. "Should I regret my offer?" His lips brushed hers in the lightest of kisses.

Sexual tension dug in its claws and for an instant she was tempted to seize him by the ears and grind their mouths together, their bodies. She stared up at him with bemusement.

How did he do this to her with barely a touch?

"Sweetheart, should I worry?"

Tomasine grinned sweetly. "Hell yes. Of course you should."

"That's what I thought." He dipped his head and closed the distance between their lips. It was a slow mating of mouths. Just lips at first. Nibbling kisses that taunted and teased and made her hunger for more. Then he licked one corner of her mouth and pushed the tip of his tongue inside. A moan escaped her, the echoes of his move rippling low in her pussy. She stirred restlessly but maintained her fierce grip on the wooden bars that ran the length of her headboard. He repeated the move—a slow thrust of his tongue into her mouth. Urgent hunger dug in its claws and her pulse raced as she waited for his next move.

His lips traveled across to her ear. He blew softly, and when she didn't protest, he nibbled on her earlobe and sucked it into his mouth. Not quite what she'd expected but interesting and strangely erotic. He swirled his tongue round the contours of her ear and flicked his tongue inside without warning. Tomasine jolted. *Oh yes.* Definitely erotic. She gasped and gripped the wooden slats a bit harder.

Where would he touch next? She peeked through lowered lashes but his expression revealed little. He shifted his body weight, the mattress moving and the bed creaking. She sucked in a deep breath and caught a hint of green and the outdoors along with the perfume she now loathed.

He tugged the top dome button of her jeans and unfastened the rest of the buttons with an ease that left her a trifle perturbed. She didn't like the idea of other women in his life, which was unfair since she'd been married and had a child. It would be terrible if Felix resented Sylvie.

"Lift," he ordered.

Tomasine raised her hips and he peeled the denim down her legs, leaving her clad in pale blue panties and her white bra. She wondered if he'd noticed her lingerie didn't match. Too bad. Bernard was gone. She never had to match lingerie again.

Felix tossed the jeans aside and placed a kiss on her kneecap. If she'd thought things might progress from there, she was disappointed. He headed south. Way south to grip one of her feet in his work-rough hands. He massaged lightly, stroking her arches and toes until she relaxed into the mattress with a contented purr. Talented and sexy.

"Are you ticklish?" he asked.

"No." Intrigued, she wondered why he wanted to know and then the next minute, he raised her foot to his mouth and sucked on her toes, one after the other. A buzz of anticipation thrummed through her along with wide-eyed astonishment. Flames of heat flickered up her legs. Not her favorite thing, but interesting. "I think I need more direct stimulation."

Felix released her toe with an audible pop and grinned at her. "Just getting acquainted. I didn't see much of you last night."

"Your eyesight is as good as mine. You saw plenty."

"Let's say I'm happy to revisit." He kneaded her calf muscle and made gradual forays up her inner thigh. She gave a happy sigh. This was looking better. Much better. Felix parted her legs so he could kneel between them. The man was still dressed in jeans and T-shirt while she was almost naked. *Again*. He wore an intent expression, his concentration on her and for her alone.

His careful attention, his teasing fingers and abrasive tongue roused her femininity. Every one of the sexual yearnings, pushed to the far reaches of her mind, popped to life like magical genies and roared at her.

Felix nibbled the soft skin of her inner thigh. She winced at the suddenness of it but he soothed the sting away with a sweep of his tongue. Rough yet sensual, she recalled the way his tongue felt lapping at her juices and curling around her clit. Restlessly she stirred, her gaze beseeching him for action.

He grinned. "Patience, sweetheart."

He lifted her, cupping her bottom with his hands and pressing his nose against the crotch of her panties. Tomasine's breath caught as she watched his face. When his lashes lifted, she saw the glittering desire. Their gazes meshed, held and the breathable air whooshed from the bedroom. Frissons of excitement pummeled her while she waited for his next move.

"You want me," he said in a husky voice.

"Yes." It was nothing less than the truth.

"Good because you belong to me." His face bore an untamed quality but he didn't frighten her because she suspected he might be right. When they were together, it felt as if a missing part of her slotted into place.

Tomasine bit her lip to keep from blurting her agreement. Early days yet. Her daughter and Gina came first. Always.

He inhaled while he stared at her, and a shudder racked his muscular frame.

Tomasine thought he might rip off her panties. She wanted them gone, but instead he leaned over and dipped his tongue into her navel. He licked in broad strokes, sweeping in a clockwise direction, circling inward. A quiver of sensation streaked straight to her core. She gasped as he repeated the move, her body tingling, her breasts prickling against the cotton confines of her bra.

"Too many clothes." Both of them.

"Patience." A hint of a smile twitched his lips at her impatient huff. "Turn over for me."

"I'll have to release my hands."

"Yeah, but you won't be able to touch because you'll be lying on your tummy."

"Humph," Tomasine muttered, but she obeyed his order. So far everything he'd done had felt great. Frustrating yet seductive. Only a fool would turn from whatever lay in store for her. Without haste, she flopped onto her stomach. Silence reigned in the bedroom. Her skin prickled and her feline senses confirmed his scrutiny.

"The undergarments need to go."

Oh yes please. Her bra sagged when he unfastened the hook-and-eye closure, and her breasts eased into a more comfortable position. She waited eagerly for him to whisk off the garment and touch her aching body. It didn't happen. Instead he tugged off her panties and tossed them aside. Felix grasped her upper thighs and parted her legs, allowing the cool air to whisper across her exposed sex. The sensation was exquisite against her heated body, while knowing he studied her hidden folds stoked her arousal higher. Heat gathered in her face as she imagined his expression. The one thing that could make it better would be if he touched. Beseeching words crowded her throat but she choked them back.

The mattress moved beneath his weight, then he stroked his fingers across one buttock cheek ever so softly. With lazy circles, he trailed his hand over her bottom. It was soothing and arousing and still frustrating. He manipulated her flesh, alternating kneading moves with unexpected but playful smacks that sent licks of heat straight to her pussy.

Smack. Smack. Smack.

She writhed on the bed. "Felix. Please." Her bottom glowed with heat while increasingly urgent hunger clawed at her control. She was so ready for his possession—his cock plunging deep...filling her pussy.

"Please what?" Laughter laced his tone. He sucked and he nibbled. He stroked and smacked again.

Tomasine squirmed, aware of her arousal. She shifted her weight, eagerly waiting for his next move. Her breasts ached for attention while the simmering need he'd built in her already rose a notch. A sharp tap on her buttocks wrenched a throaty groan free.

"Are you okay?" Felix turned her so she stared up at him. He glanced at her face for an instant longer as if reassuring himself before he tugged her loose bra down her arms.

Tomasine frowned as Felix sat back on his heels to study her breasts. They were large given her petite frame and sagged a little after breastfeeding her daughter. He touched the tip of one nipple with the back of his hand and watched it contract. "Beautiful."

"Thanks," she whispered, treasuring the rare compliment. "You can touch, if you want."

Oh yeah. He intended to touch and a bit more. Felix suppressed a swallow and the need for haste. His cock and balls burned with desperation, the reason he remained dressed. He knew the moment his clothes came off, he'd need to thrust into her hard and fast, forgoing other preliminaries. This time was for her, for discovering what she enjoyed, for exploring and appeasing his curiosity.

Her pretty coral-colored nipples had pulled tight. Felix ran his finger along the underside of one breast from base to the edge of her areola and watched her reaction. She jerked, her breathing hard. He repeated the move and heard the catch in her breath.

"Hands above your head," he whispered, waiting until she followed the order before touching her again. Once her fingers curled around the bars of the headboard, he cupped and lifted both breasts, massaging the undersides with a gentle circular motion. Her eyes fluttered closed and she relaxed under his ministrations.

Watching her open reactions, the change in her body and smelling the rich scent of her arousal was pure torment but also a revelation at how much he cared for her already. In the past he would have sped to consummation. The need to give as well as receive was something new. And daunting because it heralded a different chapter in his life. He wouldn't be alone any longer.

Felix bent his head to kiss and nibble at the full globes. He smelled warm shifter female and the clean scent of soap with only the suggestion of the perfume. He explored every inch of her breasts with his mouth, starting at the plump undersides before working toward the areola and finally, his mouth closed over the tip. With gentle suction, he teased her and drove himself toward madness.

He felt the rising tension in her body, the increased heart rate and soft purring that signaled pleasure. He let her nipple pop from his mouth and studied the shining wetness before glancing up at her. They stared at each other and it was easy to read the pleading in her expression.

Although tempted, he stuck to his game plan. He wanted her addicted to him, to their lovemaking, craving him so much she'd never consider leaving Middlemarch. Selfish perhaps—yet necessary. Felix knew he'd never survive in a city or another country town. A visit was manageable but nothing more. He'd tried and almost suffocated living amongst the sheer numbers of nameless people and tall, closed-in buildings. He liked the familiarity of family and friends in Middlemarch. He liked his job as a farmer, tending land and animals.

"Are you going on strike?"

The snippy tone brought a grin. It seemed as though his plan to turn himself into an addiction was working. "I'm pondering what to do next."

"I can draw you a map."

Felix suppressed a smirk and started paying attention to her other breast. The second his mouth closed over her nipple she ceased her impatient sighs and relaxed. He loved her demands and her tart mouth, her independent streak. A typical cat—aloof and solitary, sneaky and cunning. His amusement dispersed. All qualities that helped a shifter stay alive in this modern world.

He drew a fraction harder and the loud purr that rumbled deep in her throat echoed in his mind. She was responsive and open in her loving despite being so wary in her everyday life.

Felix gave her nipple one final thorough lick and let go, then moved back down the bed.

"About time."

Felix chuckled and arranged himself between her parted legs. He stroked the flats of his hands over her pelvic bone and her upper thighs, letting her get used to the idea he was going to become more intimate. He lifted her legs and placed them over his shoulders so her pussy was at the perfect level for exploration. Felix caressed the entire area very lightly, smiling at her musical purr.

"More," she demanded in a hoarse voice.

Felix pressed open-mouthed kisses to the skin of her upper thigh and breathed warm air onto it, skirting her vulva. Her legs relaxed as he continued to explore, parting her pubic hair and brushing his finger over her folds. A soft groan erupted as he delicately opened the outer lips and breathed on her exposed flesh.

"Felix, you're torturing me." A soft protest.

"Yeah."

"Stop," she said in a sharp voice.

"You want me to stop?" *Shit*.

"No. No! Don't stop. I meant you should cease teasing. I'm dying here."

"Glad you cleared that up," Felix said, his heart still pumping to expel the alarm that had seized him on hearing the first stop.

He increased his pace, skimming his fingers lightly without touching her clit. Her breathing grew choppy and the spicy scent of her arousal more arousing to him. Each light flicking move, each touch brought more juices to the entrance of her vagina. He dipped a finger into her and she thrust against it, pushing him deeper.

Amused at her impatience, he continued his slow exploration even though it was killing him. Withdrawing his finger, he played her swollen clit. His hand trembled, making him grimace. He had the control of a green kitten who hadn't gone through his first change.

Felix arranged her lower body on the mattress, stood and ripped off his shirt. His socks, jeans and boxers followed with quick dispatch. Pausing to grab a condom, he ripped open the packet and rolled it on his painfully erect cock. Seconds later he pushed into her with one seamless thrust.

Fully seated, he froze. "Ah hell. That feels good." If he moved, he was going to lose control. He started counting backward from ten to one. Didn't help.

"Can I touch you now?"

"Yeah. Do your worst." Felix savored the warm grip of her channel as it flexed around his dick. Hell, he'd died and landed in heaven. Her arms came around him, holding him to her as if she were afraid he'd stop. No chance of that. He withdrew and pushed back inside, setting up a seductive rhythm. They both sighed their pleasure. Tomasine drew his head down and claimed his lips in a rough kiss. Her tongue pushed into his mouth and his cock jumped. Felix quickened his thrusts and hoped he'd prepared her enough. He couldn't hold on much longer.

"You close?" he demanded.

"So now you decide to hurry," she mocked.

Even though it killed him, Felix withdrew from her totally and they stared at each other for a long moment. Dismay filled her eyes. He wanted to laugh even though his balls ached something fierce.

"I can go slow again." A lie. He hoped she didn't call him on it. He might implode if he kept up this pace. All the cold showers in the world wouldn't cure the gnawing ache in his balls, his mind. His soul.

"Clock is ticking," she countered sweetly. "Leo will arrive back with the girls."

She had a point. Felix guided himself back inside her pussy and they both let out a purr of contentment. No mucking around this time. Firm and steady strokes propelled him toward release. Felix placed one hand beneath her butt to deepen the strokes. He felt a flutter, the faintest clamping down on his cock. A sigh followed by a loud purr. Felix stopped trying to hold back. His deep strokes became rapid, setting off a more intense sensation. It started in his balls, growing bigger, becoming more. His heart pounded like a base drum. The bed creaked in protest, the headboard thumping the wall with each thrust.

Tomasine dug her fingernails into his back. She froze, letting him do the work. He felt her contractions and heard her dark moan of pleasure. It ended on a scream, bringing a proud smirk to his face. He thrust once. Twice. The third time did the trick, turning the unbearable tension into an explosion. A guttural moan ripped from his throat. Semen spewed from his cock in powerful jets that shook his body. Blistering waves of sensation crashed over him and gradually receded. He collapsed, their sweat-sheened bodies clinging together in the after throes of orgasm.

"About time you finished," a voice came through the wall.

"Go away, Leo," Felix muttered, not wanting to move.

"He could hear?" Tomasine said in horror.

"I'd be surprised if the whole of Middlemarch didn't hear," Leo called.

His brother was grinning. He could hear it in Leo's voice. Felix would have thumped the humor from his younger brother but he was too contented to move. Leo could go tease someone else.

"The girls," Tomasine gasped. "Where are the girls?"

Good point. He wouldn't want to corrupt two young shifters.

"I left the girls with Emily. They're baking gingerbread men and macaroni cheese. Saber is with them so I thought it would be okay." Leo paused then added, "I can go back and get them if you want." The words didn't ring with eagerness and Felix wondered if Gina was making him uncomfortable with her flirting.

"What do you want to do?" Felix smoothed the hair from her forehead so he could see her face clearly. "It's up to you."

The battle was a hard fought one. He saw it on her face. She didn't want the girls out of her sight but she was reluctant to create a drama from nothing. While waiting for her decision, he stroked one breast, noting the fine network of veins beneath the surface. He dipped his head and took her nipple into his mouth, tonguing it gently.

"Are you two listening? If I don't get a decision soon, I'm coming in," Leo said.

"What time should I pick them up?" Tomasine said.

Relief crawled through Felix. Trusting them to keep the girls safe was a big step for her.

"Emily said you were to come out to the farm for dinner and pick them up there."

Tomasine tensed beneath him and Felix mentally cursed his sister-in-law.

"I didn't put that very well," Leo said. "She told me to ask you to dinner and if that suited, she will take them home with her after work. Is that okay?"

Felix let go of her nipple. "You can say no, if that makes you feel easier. We're not going to snob you if you have other plans."

"I...no, that's okay."

Felix nodded. "Did you get that, Leo?"

"Yeah. Catch ya later," his brother said. They heard retreating footsteps and the slam of the door when the wind caught it. Minutes later, they heard the ute.

"Looks as if I'm trapped here with you," Felix said. "Anything in particular you want to do?"

Although she smiled, he noticed the pucker of worry on her brow. He made a promise to himself. Somehow he would chase the shadows from her life. Tomasine Brooks and her girls deserved a full and safe life full of love and laughter. At the very least, he could give her that.

Chapter 5

Devious Schemes

Joseph Magumbo trembled, savoring the warm feminine limbs that twined around him. He grasped the large breasts of the woman he was fucking, one in each hand, and squeezed hard. She winced but remained silent. She knew better. A second woman caressed his butt with her warm, soft hands and pushed a lubed finger inside his anus. Joseph shuddered helplessly at the sensual assault. God, it felt good. The delicate brush of fingers against his prostate gland pushed him toward the climax that shimmered just out of reach. He thrust once, the tension clawing at his control.

"More," he ordered in a hoarse voice.

The woman below him bit his shoulder hard enough to draw blood while the woman behind shoved another finger into his rectum. The larger intrusion combined with another bite from the female beneath him and one last thrust pushed him into a spectacular release. His cock jerked with explosive contractions, semen shooting from him in hard blasts. Joseph's eyes squeezed shut. A moan of pleasure echoed in the dimly lit bedroom.

He collapsed on the woman beneath him. When the pleasure receded he stirred, impatiently shrugging off the woman at his back. He pulled his wet cock from the woman beneath him, stood to remove the condom and grabbed a handful of tissues to clean up.

He frowned at the two women, one black and one white, sprawled on the white silk sheets of the king-size bed. Before the sex, he'd appreciated the contrast of their skin tones against the linen but now that he was done, he wanted them gone.

"Out. Tell Lucas and Robert I wish to see them." His quiet voice held arrogance. Power. They feared him—it showed in their prompt response to his order. One of the women picked up her clothes and started to dress but the other noted his scowl and nudged her friend. After a quick glance at his impassive face, they scuttled from his bedroom suite like frightened bugs. Bah! They were part of his clan, his to use as he wished. They weren't any better than insects.

Joseph prowled from the bedroom into the en suite, the cream carpet thick and luxurious beneath his bare feet. A bit different from his time growing up on the savannah and living in a mud hut. Glass surrounded the shower while a gleaming spa bath, large enough for two, filled a corner. A brass pot containing a lacy green fern sat on a shelf near the bath along with a dish of perfumed soaps. He'd earned the luxuries. Persuading Bernard to move their close friends and family to the city was the best decision he'd made. It had helped him attain power and wealth and set the stage for his takeover.

A feral grin spread across his face as he reached into the shower to turn on the water. Multiple showerheads sprang to

89

life and steam soon filled the cubicle. Joseph stepped beneath the needlelike spray and gave a groan of pleasure when the warm water beat on his shoulders. Nothing better than a good fuck followed by a shower and a gourmet meal.

And it would be even better once they found the woman.

Eliminate the final risk.

Joseph rubbed sandalwood-scented soap over his chest and gritted his teeth when he considered the search. Why the fuck was it taking so long? He'd summoned his men to explain. They'd better have answers because he was tired of excuses. He scrubbed the sweat and sex from his body and washed away the soap.

Not the relaxing shower he'd envisioned.

Joseph grabbed a white towel from the rack near the shower. He dabbed away the worst of the water and checked the bite on his shoulder. The flow of blood had ceased but he made a mental note to ring reception for first-aid supplies. After shrugging into a white toweling robe, he padded back into the bedroom.

The soft murmur of voices came from the lounge area of the suite. Joseph sauntered from the bedroom to deal with his men.

He wanted results.

Robert and Lucas came to attention the instant he entered. They sprang to their feet and watched him warily. As well they should.

"I want to know if you've found the woman yet."

Robert glanced at Lucas before answering. "We tracked her and the kid as far as Melbourne in Australia. Have some promising leads. We think she might have gone to New Zealand."

"Think?" Joseph exploded across the room and backhanded the man across the jaw.

Robert's head snapped back. He staggered off balance before righting himself and wiping the back of his hand across his mouth. Blood showed on his hand and trickled from his lip where Joseph's heavy gold ring had caught and torn his skin.

Satisfaction swept through Joseph. His special secret weapon. It worked every time.

Lucas stepped out of range despite his bulk and larger physique. He knew better than to tug the pissed leopard's tail. "We have people in New Zealand now following up leads. Our people are professionals. They will find her."

"I want results. The woman must die." Joseph pictured the petite woman in his mind—her luscious body and sun-kissed skin, ripe for the picking. His hand swept down his torso, jolting his growing erection. He'd offered her everything. She'd laughed and turned him down. Laughed at him! His lips tightened in determination and he eyed his men with impatience. What the hell was so difficult about finding and subduing one small female?

"I will contact our liaison for the latest progress," Lucas said.

Robert's brow crinkled. "What about the kid?"

Joseph walked across the broad expanse of cream carpet, past a cream leather two-seater to a glass-and-chrome sideboard. A silver tray set on the glass top, bore six whisky tumblers and a decanter full of the best Scottish whisky money could buy.

"My cousin's spawn should have been drowned at birth. I want them both dead. Set the assassins on her. I don't want messy entanglements to get in the way of making the crown officially mine."

Lucas nodded respectfully, hiding his real opinion from his cousin. "It will be done, Joseph."

After a glance at Robert and a quick jerk of his head signaling they should leave, Lucas walked across the thick carpet heading for the door. His breath eased out once he was safely out of the hotel suite and still alive.

Joseph acted deranged and unreasonable.

Instead of moving on, cementing his position of power gained after the massacre of their enemies, he'd become fixated on his cousin's wife.

Hell, they weren't even sure the woman was still alive. Identification of the bodies in the village had proved difficult since the scavengers had ravaged the site before their arrival. It was possible they were chasing a phantom female across the world despite Joseph's opinion to the contrary.

Robert wiped the blood from his gashed lip and glanced uneasily at Lucas. "What are we going to do? We don't know for sure if the queen is alive or not."

"I know. Have we heard back from all our contacts?"

"Yeah, everyone except the original assassin Joseph set to watch and take out Bernard. We haven't heard from her in over two years. She was the best I've ever seen. The woman never gave up once she'd taken a contract. One hundred percent success rate."

Lucas frowned deep in thought. "When we failed to hear from her, it was assumed she died in the massacre but I suppose it's worth attempting a contact just in case. Yeah, good point. We shouldn't presume anything. I'll take steps to establish contact and see what happens."

*F*our weeks later

After Tomasine's confession, Felix made it a point to chip away at her closed emotions. He wanted it all, just as Saber had with Emily. His feelings were clear to him, but Tomasine still acted wary. Patience required—the shadows he glimpsed in her confirmed his need for stealth and persistence.

Felix crawled from the warm bed and dressed, at ease in the dark room. That was the other thing he hadn't been able to change. Tomasine wouldn't let him stay overnight because of Sylvie and Gina. Although he spent hours with her and the girls, she was scrupulous about appearances and her reputation. It would set a bad example, she said.

Fully dressed, Felix bent over Tomasine and brushed a lingering kiss over her mouth. A sexy little whimper emerged from deep in her throat. Still asleep though. He smiled and tiptoed from the room. It was good to see her looking so peaceful and the fact that she didn't wake and grab for the knife she kept under the mattress told him she was coming to trust him.

She mightn't realize it but they were meant to be together. The thought brought a sentimental lump to his throat. Hell, he sympathized with Saber and the problems he'd had with Emily.

He would never laugh at his brothers' attempts to woo and win their mates again.

Felix crept down the short passage to the front door, avoiding the creaking board outside Gina's bedroom. Gina made him laugh and her obvious crush on his brother was cute, even though it made Leo uncomfortable. He unlocked the door, slipped outside and relocked it with the key Tomasine had given him.

He'd taken to leaving his vehicle parked out of sight behind the pub even though it was ten minutes from Tomasine's house. Felix strode through the darkness, alert for anything out of the ordinary. It was more to soothe Tomasine's fears but he enjoyed the brisk walk back to his vehicle. Sometimes he shifted and ran back to the farm but tonight he'd driven after promising Saber he'd pick up the drench that had been delivered from Dunedin. They needed it for first thing in the morning, before the rural delivery lady could deliver it in her mail van.

He headed into town, taking care to tread silently despite his pace. The main street of Middlemarch lay in darkness apart from the security lights glowing from the garage, small supermarket and the post office. The bleat from the goat tethered on the road frontage outside the Gibson property broke the silence.

Felix tensed without warning, every sense on high alert. It wasn't something he heard or saw, more gut instinct that made him slide deep into the shadows cast by a pine tree.

His heart thumped with apprehension. During the last month, he hadn't heard or seen anyone on his nightly jaunts back to the farm. He peered from his hiding place, inching out because the hair at the back of his neck prickled in foreboding. Someone was out there. He couldn't see them yet and it might be innocent, but given Tomasine's worries, he decided to err on the side of caution.

He waited for five minutes. Ten. Tension swirled in his gut. Was he overreacting? Five minutes later, Felix decided he was alone until a flash caught his eye. Despite the risk of being seen, he slipped from the shadows and prowled toward the spot.

Identify the danger. Eliminate it. No way did he intend to frighten Tomasine and risk losing her. He sensed she would flee at the slightest provocation. A scowl twisted his lips. She needed to confide in him instead of keeping secrets.

Felix slipped into the murk by the supermarket and studied the darkness, his vicinity. Then he saw them.

It was a person, dressed totally in black. Slender. Cautious. Studying the shadows as carefully as he did.

Then the person turned toward him.

A woman.

A stranger.

Felix grunted, appreciating her stark blonde beauty. Curiosity rose in him. Questions. What was she doing skulking around Middlemarch in the early hours of the morning? While not against the law, it was bloody suspicious and in light of Tomasine's concerns, he needed to learn the woman's purpose.

She disappeared for an instant, swallowed by the gloom. Felix caught sight of her again as she flitted across the street. He followed.

Alert and experienced, the woman kept glancing over her shoulder so Felix dropped back, letting the distance between them grow. One moment she sneaked in front of him and the next she'd disappeared. A few minutes later, the throb of an engine over to his right made Felix hustle in that direction.

He was too late.

A late-model bike zipped from a narrow driveway near the railway station, speeding so fast Felix missed the number plate. He pulled up by the railway station ticket office, cursing under his breath as the deep rumble of the bike receded. The woman's appearance might be innocent but it wouldn't hurt to step up security.

Felix turned back to where he'd left his SUV parked and drove home. He pulled up outside the family homestead and decided to grab a few hours' sleep before talking to Saber.

Three and a half hours later he walked into the kitchen to find Saber, Emily and Leo already seated around the kitchen table, coffee mugs in hand, discussing plans for drenching the cattle and the possibility of attending a sale to buy sheep.

"I'm worried about the feed situation for the stock," Saber said.

Leo frowned. "You think we should wait until spring and the new growth before we buy more sheep?"

Felix grabbed a mug from the cupboard near the coffeemaker, poured himself a cup and dropped into an empty seat. "I saw a stranger in town this morning."

Emily's gaze speared to him. "What sort of a stranger? We need details."

"A woman. It's probably nothing but Tomasine is so wary. I thought it was strange to find her loitering around the area at that time of the morning. She escaped on a motor bike before I could note the number plate."

"A woman?" Leo zeroed in on the one thing that made Felix think his doubts might be unfounded.

"You shouldn't underestimate a woman," Emily said indignantly. "We're capable of anything. We were the first country in the world to gain the vote for women and we've had three female prime ministers, you know."

"Quite right, sweetheart," Saber said, winking at his mate. "We were merely surprised." He turned back to Felix. "What made you think the woman might be a threat?"

Felix frowned, thinking back to the moment when he'd seen her, trying to analyze his conclusions. "Nothing concrete. Gut instinct."

Saber nodded. "I'll inform the council elders. We'll alert everyone and keep a closer eye on Tomasine and her girls. Maybe you could persuade them to move in here. They'd be easier to watch."

"I've asked Tomasine already. She refused. She wants to maintain her independence." Felix's jaw tightened as he replayed the conversation in his head. He'd wanted to shake her into agreement. He'd wanted to make love to her so well that she'd yearn for him, need him and be desperate to spend her days with him. Nothing he said had changed her mind. She still withheld her trust and it hurt, especially since she was the one his feline craved.

His mate.

Emily reached over the table to pat his hand. Felix felt his throat tighten at the understanding in her gaze. "Give her time,

Felix. She's been on her own, responsible for two girls and she's trying to keep them safe. Tomasine needs time to trust us."

Emily made it seem easy but he wanted to make their relationship permanent. He wanted to help raise Sylvie and Gina and maybe have more children.

"Have you told Tomasine?" Leo asked.

Felix shook his head. "I haven't talked to her today." Part of him wanted to protect Tomasine and hide his worries from her. He wanted to keep the information from her but knew it was wrong. "I'll head over there now and take Sylvie to school and Gina to the bus. Tomasine and I can talk once the girls are safe at school."

"Give me a description of the woman and her bike so I can tell everyone," Saber said. "Our friends and neighbors will want to help."

"Now that they've recovered from the shock of her being a shifter," Leo said, his tone dry. "I swear, some of them have earmarked the two girls as mates for their boys. You're going to have boys crowding your girls once you and Tomasine are settled."

Felix grimaced but appreciated his brother's tact and assumption that he and Tomasine had a future. He accepted the notebook and pen Leo snared off the kitchen counter. After thinking back to the previous night, he scribbled down blonde hair. Tall. Slender. Dressed in black. Bike—dark blue or black. No—black. Powerful. Felix scowled at the details before he handed them to Saber. It wasn't much.

A knock at the door heralded Felix. Tomasine could tell by the double knock followed by the long pause and two more rapid knocks. Felix's code.

"Felix is here." Gina glanced toward the door, her chubby face sparkling with eagerness. "I wonder if Leo came with him. Did you hear one set of footsteps or two?"

"I'm not sure." The thought brought trepidation. They were slipping. Relaxing their safety measures. She couldn't afford to let her guard slide into casual. While Felix didn't believe her fears of the danger, she knew better. She glanced at the clock on the wall above the table. She worried about the girls home alone. "Sylvie, hurry with your breakfast or we'll be late. If you're finished, go and clean your teeth. Gina, do you have your assignment?"

"All ready to go, Tom." She bustled about, cleaning the small kitchen as she did every morning. "Do you have any assignments today?"

"I thought I might drive out to Sutton Lake and write a piece on that since it's unique. The lone inland salt lake in New Zealand, I heard." Tomasine opened the door and both Felix and Leo stepped inside. Her stomach started to flutter straightaway, her nipples pulled tight and she was very aware of the way her clothes draped across her body. Her mind slid to sex and Felix removing them for her piece by piece, kissing each part of her body he bared.

"Hi." Felix walked straight up to her and kissed her. She felt his touch clear to her toes—heck, her toes curled.

"Ah-um." Gina cleared her throat loudly. "If we don't leave now, I'll miss the bus. You're not dressed."

"I'll run the girls to school for you," Leo said.

"Good," Gina said, fluttering her eyelashes.

When Tomasine pulled away from Felix, she noticed Gina had applied a little makeup but didn't say anything to embarrass the girl. Leo was universally popular, and she trusted him enough to take the girls to school even though it didn't stop her worrying. "Are you sure it's no trouble?"

Leo grinned and edged away from Gina. His tactful silence regarding Gina's enthusiasm and bumbling attempts to flirt made her like Felix's brother even more. "We decided to muster the stock for drenching later this afternoon so I'm at your disposal."

"Thanks." Tomasine stooped to kiss Sylvie and gave Gina a hug. "Be good."

"Always," Gina said, casting her a cheeky grin. "Do you have a girlfriend?" she asked Leo.

Tomasine caught Leo rolling his eyes before opening the door to usher the two girls out. She bit back a smile.

"Do you have a girlfriend?" Sylvie asked, taking Leo's hand. "Gina wants to be your girlfriend. She likes you."

"Shut up, Sylvie," Gina snapped.

Tomasine could see Gina's cheeks were hot enough to act as a breakfast griddle while Sylvie reminded her of a mischievous imp. She couldn't help grinning at the slice of normality, the teasing between siblings.

"Sylvie, that's enough," she said, attempting to rein in her amusement. It wouldn't do for Gina to catch her laughter. "Be good for Leo." She bent to kiss her daughter, smiled encouragingly at Gina, made sure they had their bags and books and waved to them from the doorstep. "I see Gina scored the front seat." Instead of a return grin, Felix remained serious.

"We need to talk."

"What? You're not going to rush me off to the bedroom?" Her attempt at humor fell flat, and she dropped onto a chair in the dining room. Her gut churned on seeing his expression, his hesitation. Surely, he wasn't going to ask her to marry him, to mate? Although tempted, she couldn't tie herself to one man. Cripes, how was she going to handle him if he asked her to mate?

Felix dropped into the seat opposite her. "Last night I was walking to my car and saw a strange woman, someone I didn't recognize."

Oh god. Tomasine bounded to her feet, her gaze darting around the lounge and kitchen area and the portion of the back lawn she could see from where she stood. She searched for the stranger, cast out her feline senses. Illogical, but adrenaline pumped through her veins along with the need for flight.

She panted for quick air, tried to shove down her panic. *Keep it together. You can do this.* "What did she look like? Where did she go?" Her sharp tone verbalized her panic despite her attempt at calm.

"Sit. It might be nothing but I thought you should know. I followed the woman and lost her. She was blonde. Slender. She wore black and rode a motorbike."

"I'll pack." Tomasine fought to think, her mind busy as she determined which of her plans to use. Where to run, the best place to hide, given her current knowledge. Fatigue struck. *So tired of running*. She shoved her exhaustion aside and focused.

North. She'd head north, catch the ferry over Cook Strait to Wellington. Perhaps Auckland since it was a bigger city. Although she disliked cities, it was easier to lose followers amongst the mass of people. "Yes, I'll pack and leave as soon as the girls arrive home from school." It would take that long to make the travel arrangements.

Felix jumped to his feet, his larger frame looming over her. "Pack? Why?"

Tomasine attempted to push past his immobile body, shoving him in the ribs when he refused to move. "I can't stay here. Out of my way. Don't you understand? If they catch us, the three of us are as good as dead. They don't leave survivors." She pushed Felix again, terror clawing her mind. *It wasn't fair.* She'd been happy in Middlemarch. The girls were settled and doing well in school.

She'd thought—hoped—they'd stop chasing her once they realized she had no intention of returning to Africa. *Ever.*

"Tomasine, listen to yourself." Felix grasped her upper arms and shook her slightly until he grabbed her attention. "I saw one stranger. Her appearance might be innocent. Saber is passing the word amongst the shifter community. Everyone will watch for anything suspicious. Running again won't solve anything. The girls are happy. Leaving will unsettle them." Felix relaxed his grip on her arms, not wanting to hurt her. And he'd noticed that although she was talking about fleeing, she hadn't hesitated to manhandle him despite his size. She didn't fear him. That tiny acceptance offered hope—the knowledge she was coming to trust him. He could work on the rest. "Saber suggested you and the girls move in with us at the homestead. There's plenty of room since the twins are living in Dunedin now."

"No, I—"

"If you leave, I'm going with you." Amusement flooded him when her mouth fell open in shock.

"You told me you'd never leave Middlemarch, that you'd tried it and hated city life. When I leave, I'll head for a city since it's easier to blend."

"I will be with you, no matter where you go." Felix didn't verbalize his reasons, knowing she wasn't ready to hear the truth. It was true he couldn't see himself living anywhere other than Middlemarch. His attempts at living in the city had made him unhappy. But she was his mate. The thought of her leaving twisted his gut. His heart raced as he battled with the urge to grab her and run to the homestead. He'd give up everything to be with her. If Tomasine thought to walk from his life, she needed to rethink her plans.

Chapter 6

Unwilling Trust

Two hours later, after much discussion and argument, Felix ushered Tomasine from his SUV toward the silent homestead, his hand at the small of her back. Her expression hovered in a scowl but running wouldn't help. She couldn't keep fleeing forever.

Felix directed her to the front door. Low and sprawling, the homestead was made from local schist. Emily had enticed Saber into planting flowers to add color and contrast with the gray stone of the house. Now under Emily's supervision, the lavender edging the narrow concrete path leading to the front door was neatly trimmed and tubs of white and blue flowers—Felix had no idea what they were but they looked okay—flanked the door. Once summer arrived, Emily said they had to dig new garden beds and she'd already started a vegetable garden out the back of the house. Felix and his brothers preferred meat, but they all ate vegetables to keep Emily happy.

Felix opened the door and stepped into the hall. He bent to take off his boots and Tomasine followed suit. A coatrack stood in the corner, another of Emily's changes to keep their coats tidy. The faint drift of lemon polish caught his attention as he led Tomasine down the carpeted passage to his bedroom. The house always smelled clean these days. Times were changing.

"I'll show you your rooms and come back for your bags. We can pick up the girls later."

"But what if—"

"The girls will be safe at school. The bus driver is a shifter and one of the teachers at the primary school is also shifter. If anyone sees anything suspicious, they'll alert us."

Felix shouldered open another door and stood aside to let Tomasine enter. "This is our bedroom."

"I'm not—"

"You're my mate and the sooner you accept that fact the better." Felix dropped the bag he was carrying on the floor and tugged her resisting body into his arms. He gave her a quick squeeze before pushing her away to look deep into her eyes. "I'm not going to force the mating mark on you—I would never do that, but I want you. I want to spend time with you and keep you close. That means sleeping with you."

Tomasine scowled, her nose and brow wrinkling with worry. "But the girls—it's setting a bad example."

Felix smiled—a tender smile of affection—and ran his fingers across her lips until she stopped frowning. He tugged on her ponytail. "That's better. We don't want to risk the wind changing. You might end up looking like a gargoyle."

Tomasine let out an indignant snort. "Stop changing the subject. I don't want to give the girls the wrong idea."

"It's not as if we're having sex in front of them. I understand having the girls around makes our relationship different. The girls are part of you, part of your life. When we mate, the girls become my family and responsibility. I know you're a package deal. I like your girls. Together we'll be a family." They'd fill a hole inside him, one he hadn't been aware of until Emily entered their lives. Felix didn't have experience with children though he was willing to learn. He *wanted* to learn.

Tomasine glanced up at him, her gaze still full of apprehension. "I'm frightened."

"I know, sweetheart. But please, give this a chance. Give us a chance. I know you don't trust me enough to tell me of your past yet. That's okay. Trust takes time. You can ask me anything you like about our family, about Middlemarch, and I'll answer."

"That's a bit risky, given I'm a reporter," Tomasine said in a dry tone, but the softening in her brown eyes told him she understood his offer of trust. "Where will the girls sleep?"

"At the other end of the passage in the twins' room."

Tomasine hesitated and Felix walked back to where she stood by his double bed. He tried not to think of the two in the same thought but it happened anyway and predictably blood filled his cock. Hell, he'd love to rip her clothes off and take her hard and fast, preferably with a little biting in the equation. He wanted to take their relationship to the next level, to mark her as his mate. He could force the issue and win, but the victory would ring hollow. He wanted her to accept him without coercion.

Tomasine chewed on her bottom lip. "What am I going to tell Sylvie? I don't want her to go through life with a fear of strangers."

"Why don't you tell her the house needs fumigating? What about the landlord? Why don't you tell her the landlord wants to fix the roof?" Felix scrutinized her face, her white teeth and the increased redness of her lip where she'd abused it. His cock jerked yet again but he knew better than to kiss her with his precarious control.

Tomasine's breasts rose and fell in a heavy sigh. She gave a grudging nod.

"What about Gina?" Felix battled the need to trail his fingers across her face. She was so tempting. Distracting. *His*.

"Gina insisted I tell her the truth from the start. My...cousin...let's just say she's older than her years. We've been through a lot together."

Felix surrendered to his craving to touch. He ran his fingers across her silky sun-kissed cheek and smoothed a lock of hair from her face. "Has Gina shifted yet? My brothers and I shifted for the first time about her age."

"She hasn't shown any signs. I've told her the symptoms to look for—the aching bones, the desire to eat more red meat and increased sensitivity of senses. That's part of the reason I chose Middlemarch. I knew there were other shifters here and the area isn't heavily built-up. There's plenty of room for shifters to run."

"Why Middlemarch? There are other colonies out there, if you know where to look."

"I know, but most are in close contact with each other. In Europe anyway. I wanted anonymity until I knew where their loyalties lay. When I was a child, I heard my parents discussing my mother's auntie. She knew a family, friends of friends, who considered immigrating here. I didn't think any more about it until I needed to hide. The rumors of the black panther sightings and the way everyone was so close-mouthed about it told me quite a bit about the community, even if they frustrated me at every turn." She wrinkled her nose at him. "I kept our identity secret because I wanted to be sure it was safe. I didn't know who to trust...I'm so used to hiding. It's become ingrained..." She trailed off and stared at her feet before glancing back at him, her expression pensive.

Tomasine was obsessed with safety and assassins. Part of him understood her need for secrecy but she wasn't alone now. He wasn't even sure he believed her farfetched stories of assassins. "Have you run while you've been here?"

"I didn't think it was safe."

The idea of not embracing the cat on a regular basis was a foreign concept. It was part of who they were and what made them different. Felix didn't need to think twice. They would change that. It was something small he could do for her.

Felix took her hand and led her down the passage to the twins' room. He opened the door and came to an abrupt halt. It was just as the twins had left it, complete with centerfold pictures plastered across the walls.

Tomasine giggled. "I think we'd better redecorate. Sylvie's into dolls and soft toys while Gina thinks that English singer—his name escapes me—is the cutest thing on Earth."

"Ah yeah. I'd forgotten Emily mentioned cleaning up first if you came to stay." Felix moved over to the posters and removed them from the cream-colored walls. A few minutes later, small pinholes were all that remained. Two single beds with dark green duvet covers sat at right angles to the door with a bedside cabinet beside each one. The furniture was battered and one of the cabinets bore twin-inspired graffiti. Felix grinned, remembering Saber's anger when the young teenage twins had used the cabinet for a game of naughts and crosses. There were also a couple of initials and mystery words that held no meaning to anyone other than them. A bank of windows looked out over the new vegetable garden. Felix opened a window to air the room and the white curtains fluttered in the soft breeze.

"We have a few hours before the girls finish school. The main town area is well covered. Any strangers about today won't have much privacy. Why don't we check out some of the outer-lying areas? We can run together if you want." Felix tacked the offer casually on the end, desperately wanting to share the feline part of themselves. Running with his mate...

Tomasine stared out the window. It was a clear and crisp winter day. Although there was no snow in the Strath Taieri valley, there were a few drifts on the Rock and Pillar range. Sudden longing assailed her. She hadn't shifted for...longer than she could remember and the idea of running with another shifter was enticing. It didn't hurt that the male was her lover either. She pushed away her misgivings about staying in Middlemarch where possible danger stalked the girls and her and attempted a smile. "Okay. Where?"

"We'll go out on the farm. There's a hill that overlooks most of the valley. We'll drive out to the old woolshed and sheep yards and go from there."

At the front door they paused to pull on their boots and retraced their footsteps to the SUV.

Tomasine climbed into the passenger seat and frowned at the door. "I can't believe you don't lock your doors."

"This is the country." Felix glanced across the cab at her, his eyes tender and full of understanding. "It's different in Middlemarch."

Tomasine wished she felt the same assurance. It was difficult with their lives at risk. By staying at the Mitchell homestead, she was placing them in danger too. She tried to quiet the annoying voices of terror that battered her mind. It was fine for Felix and his brothers to say it was safe to stay with them but Joseph...the lengths he'd go to ensure he retained control of the remaining clan and resources. A wave of apprehension accompanied the prickling awareness that foretold danger.

It was out there.

Tomasine couldn't see or hear it but sensed the stealthy stalking of the enemy. Her chest felt as though it would burst from the anxiety. The risk was too high. She would never forgive herself if Felix died because of her. She had to leave. *Tonight*.

They drove down a gravel road toward the rolling hills. She stared at the passing landscape, the outcrops of schist, the fleeting glimpses of the Taieri River and the rolling hills covered with grass and tussock. The wilderness and sparse population grew on a person. Adjusting to a city would take time. The girls would hate it. They'd disliked the studio flat in London, the hiding and subterfuge involved during the cat-and-mouse games with their hunters. She hated to remember Spain where the assassins had caught up with them. Things hadn't improved much in Singapore where the crush of humanity and the humidity had even worn on her nerves.

Having to consort with members of the underworld to sell her jewelry and arrange forged papers for her planned destination of New Zealand hadn't helped either. Australia had been a slight improvement but it was here in Middlemarch where the girls had flourished. She'd started to sleep through the night without nightmares or having to climb from bed to investigate unusual noises.

Felix pulled over on the road shoulder, not far from a ramshackle woolshed. "We can walk from here or we can shift here and head for the hills."

Tomasine surveyed the surrounding countryside. It was private with no other buildings in sight. The hills rose above them while below she saw the endless plains of the valley. A stand of pines stood out against the dull green of the paddocks. Overhead a bird soared. Her feline side strained for the same freedom, to feel the give of the earth beneath her paws. "Let's shift here. Do you leave your clothes in the car or somewhere else?"

"We have a watertight container to store our clothes at the back of the sheep yards."

Felix opened the gate for her and she walked through, waiting while he refastened the catch. Sheep grazed in the paddock they'd entered. Several of the wooly animals lifted their heads before retreating. In a neighboring paddock, a cow mooed.

"This way," Felix said.

Tomasine followed, her gaze lingering on his broad back then drifting to his butt. The desire to touch ate at her. Taste. She wanted to do that too. Tomasine sucked in a sharp breath and caught a hint of his spicy scent along with crisp mountain air and a hint of sheep. Blinking, she dispelled the sudden moisture from her eyes. She would miss him even though leaving was the right thing to do.

Felix paused at the rear of the yards. He unfastened his shirt buttons and shrugged from his woolen shirt to reveal his broad chest. She stared, storing memories. Felix was her mate. She accepted there would be no one else—not after him. It was worth the sacrifice, knowing Felix and his family would remain safe.

One of his dark brows rose in a teasing manner. His sensual lips curled to a grin. "Are you going to turn this into a strip show?"

"Merely appreciating the scenery." She shrugged her shoulders nonchalantly. Her gaze wandered across pectoral muscles and biceps toned by working on the farm. It was a good thing shifters didn't feel the cold since it meant she had plenty of skin to eyeball.

"If you don't stop ogling, we're not running anywhere."

The wicked glint in his green eyes stirred her to action. This might be the last opportunity to run for months. The city would be impossible. Yes. Run first and then sex.

Making love.

Tomasine yanked her woolen sweater over her head and tossed it on top of Felix's shirt before stooping to unlace her boots and remove her socks. She glanced up to catch his hot stare strolling across her body. She grinned, feeling better since she'd made her decision. It was for the best. Reaching behind, she flicked the clasp of her bra and let her breasts spill free. The cool breeze whispered across them, pulling her nipples tight. Liquid arousal moistened her pussy but she ignored the seductive need to mate. Instead, she stripped off her jeans and panties and stood for an instant, naked to the elements. She yanked off the elastic band confining her ponytail and shook her head. Her hair spilled around her shoulders.

Lifting her face to the sky, she reveled in the freedom of nature and pictured a sleek leopard in her mind. The familiar sense of disembodiment took over as her body started to change. Bones lengthened and cracked. A hint of pain mixed with the euphoria of rushing hormones. Her teeth grew sharp while the shape of her eyes changed. Black fur formed along her backbone and spread down her arms and legs.

She dropped to all fours and embraced the pain while the change completed. Finally, she stood in front of Felix, her long black tail swishing while her whiskers twitched.

"You're beautiful," he breathed.

Tomasine barked deep in her throat and flicked her tail across his jeans-clad legs. The wretched man had stood and gawked. He ran his hand the length of her backbone before moving to stand by her head. Without the slightest trace of fear, he scratched behind her ears. Stupid male. She could kill him with a quick flash of her front paws. He wouldn't have a chance. He continued to stroke and caress. A low purr erupted and she rubbed against his legs, almost knocking him over. She licked his hand, tasting the saltiness of his skin while his scent sank deep into her lungs.

"I guess we'd better hurry." Felix removed his boots then unzipped his jeans and slid them down his strong thighs. The rest of his clothes disappeared. Even in her cat form, she appreciated his masculine beauty. Felix placed all their clothes in a watertight container, then stood back to go through his own shift.

Tomasine blinked. One minute he was human and the next, a huge black leopard stalked toward her. He rubbed against her flanks then her head, purring loudly the entire time. Just a big ole kitty cat. She swatted him with one of her front paws and gave a low cough to remind him about the time constraints.

With one final purr, he padded past the woolshed and broke into a lope. Tomasine followed, reveling in the breeze ruffling her fur and the crisp scent of mountains and greenery, the uneven surface digging into the pads of her paws. Everything seemed brighter and smelled more pungent in feline form. She'd forgotten how much the small things such as taste, sight and scent took on a much larger meaning.

Felix headed up into the hills, increasing his speed until the trees, rocky outcrops and tussock started to blur. Tomasine slowed, unused to mad gallops through the countryside. Her sides heaved with exertion and she knew she'd suffer from sore muscles the next day. The exhilaration and freedom made the run worthwhile.

Finally, Felix halted near an outcrop of rocks shaped like a bird's head. He padded around the schist until he reached the sheltered side and stopped near a soft grassy area. He shifted, standing to tower above her. Proudly naked, his erection jutted in an obvious manner.

"Shift," he barked.

Tomasine obeyed and rose to her feet in front of him, her sides still heaving with fatigue.

"God, I need you," he muttered, seconds before his mouth slammed down on hers.

His urgency was contagious. Tomasine pressed her breasts against his naked chest, dragging her nipples across the smooth expanse of skin. He lifted her off her feet and strode across the grass without lifting his lips from hers. Their tongues tangled while her heart pumped with adrenaline, with urgency.

Felix set her on her feet in front of the outcrop, breaking their kiss, the mating of their mouths. The schist soared above their heads—a rough and formidable cliff. He lifted his head to look intently into her eyes. His face took on an edge of feral. Harsh, without an ounce of tenderness but she felt no fear.

"Turn around," he ordered. "Hands on the rock."

She stared into his green eyes. They held a storm of passion, the same tempest that thrummed through her veins. Ever so slowly she turned, maintaining eye contact until it became impossible and she stared at gray rock instead. Excitement pulsed, marching across her breasts and matching a lower ache in her sex. The breeze blew across the top of the cliff, creating a strange whistle while the rock was rough and cool beneath her palms.

Felix stepped behind her and the prickling of her skin told her of his scrutiny. She shifted her weight from foot to foot and flinched when he cupped one buttock with his callused hand.

"Widen your stance."

She obeyed, anticipation making her breathing choppy. Her pussy clenched with longing and one hand lifted from the rock to soothe an aching nipple.

"Stop that," Felix barked.

Resentful, she followed his order but slowly enough to communicate her irritation.

Felix chuckled, but it was a hard sound that bore little humor. The knowledge eased her frustration and her fingers curled into the rock while she waited for his next move.

Felix teetered on the edge of control. The craving to mate and mark her held him in its grip. His hand curled around his erection. So swollen and tight it was painful, he pumped slowly, trying to gain relief. Instead the ache intensified. His skin prickled insistently.

He had to have her.

Now.

Gasping at the urgency, he traced the crack between her buttocks and pressed a soft kiss to the muscles between her neck and shoulder. Her clean, spicy scent with its hint of shifter seeped into his lungs.

His.

Always his.

He spread her legs a fraction wider. His fingers intensified the pressure, pushing down on her perineum and easing his finger toward her pussy. Liquid moisture greeted his caress along with relief. She wanted him as much as he wanted her. Felix removed his finger and repositioned her hands so she bent at a better angle. Then he guided his cock and pushed deep into her heat. The prickling became worse as did the crazed need to mark her. Felix withdrew and slammed back into her, one hand snaking around to cup a breast. He tugged at the nipple, making her groan. She pushed against him, her flesh clenching his cock so tightly, so perfectly, he thought he might burst.

"Felix, more."

Her throaty voice enticed, her body seduced.

Man, he was a goner.

Felix retreated and surged into her welcoming warmth, faster and faster. The air wheezed from his lungs, his heart pounded. Her silky hair rippled across her shoulders with each thrust, allowing him peekaboo glimpses of the sun-kissed skin of her neck. He bent his head and licked, the salty flavor of her skin combining with the scent of cat and sex and the outdoors. Unable to bear the lack for a second longer, he licked across her shoulder. Felix thrust faster, but the faster he stroked, the closer he came to orgasm and the more he wanted to mark her skin to claim her. His canines lengthened until they protruded from beneath his lips. A growl emerged from deep in his throat.

"Bite me," she said seductively.

Bite, not mate. A subtle difference. Felix shoved aside his disappointment and dragged his tongue across the meaty part of her shoulder. His cock flexed in her channel and he groaned. God, she felt so good, her slender body quivering beneath him, her pussy gripping his cock. He nibbled, offering a touch of teeth before soothing the sting with the roughness of his tongue.

"More," she pleaded.

Her body trembled. Felix was so close he shivered himself. His balls tingled as he plunged into her again. He gripped her shoulders and rocked their bodies together. A crazed urgency gripped him now. His teeth sank into her shoulder and he held her submissive while he pounded into her pussy. Tomasine groaned. She shuddered.

"Yes!" she screamed, the sound ending on a gulp.

Each breath became difficult, harsh to his ear. He felt the tremors of her pussy, the tiny convulsions signaling her climax. He pistoned his hips one last time and fire swarmed across his body, blood crowding his cock. His eyes closed as he concentrated on the sounds, the sensations, the woman who claimed him so sweetly. One more thrust was all it took. With a violent explosion his semen burst from him in a white haze of enjoyment. Felix stiffened, his muscles locking while the pleasure continued for long, endless moments.

"Tomasine." Felix withdrew and pulled her away from the rock. He hugged her to his chest, trying to convey everything he felt by touch. His mouth slammed down on hers and a thought occurred. They hadn't used a condom.

His head jerked up and he looked down at her with a trace of panic. "We didn't use a condom."

"I know."

Shock did a number on his knees. "You could have said something."

Tomasine met his gaze for a while before glancing away. "It didn't seem important in the scheme of things."

Not important? Felix opened his mouth to dispute the fact before deciding to hold his tongue. Tomasine was his mate. If today caused a pregnancy—well, he wouldn't get upset. With a gentle finger beneath her chin, he tipped her head up for his kiss. He rubbed his mouth over hers before pushing his tongue between her lips. He explored the smoothness of her inner cheeks and the taste of her before lifting his head. Finally, he tucked a lock of hair behind her ear and smiled.

"We should go if we want to sneak around before the girls finish school. I'll race you back."

Felix shifted, wanting to laugh at her surprise but all that emerged was a deep cough. He spun and galloped off down the hill, in the direction of the sheep yards, the wind rustling through his fur. The thunder of feet behind brought a feline grin to his face. Tomasine wouldn't catch him unless he allowed it. She was too unfit and unused to running through the hills of Middlemarch. He slowed abruptly and she crashed into him. They tumbled and he let out a playful growl. She slapped him across the jaw with one of her paws and leapt out of the way. Then she trotted away with a swish of her tail.

Felix grinned after her. What a woman. His woman. His mate.

Chapter 7

A Missing Child

At three in the afternoon, they pulled up outside the primary school to wait for the final bell of the day. Felix glanced across the cab at her, his eyes liquid with heat and promises for the night to come, for other nights.

Tomasine bit back a sob. Leaving would hurt even though it was best for all of them. She hated the thought of more innocents killed in the private war between her and Joseph. Not that she wanted to fight. If he'd leave her alone, she'd gladly fade into a quiet life and not go anywhere near Africa. *Ever*.

The strident clang of the bell blared from a loudspeaker affixed to the corner of a classroom. Soon, children spilled from the open doors. Some lined up inside the gates under the supervision of a female teacher while parents collected other children at the gates. Excited laughter and chatter filled the air along with screeches and bickering between siblings fighting over who would sit in the front during the drive home.

"I'll go and collect Sylvie." Tomasine climbed from Felix's SUV and entered the school grounds to wait for Sylvie. Her daughter loved school and dawdled, which worked out fine since they needed to wait for Gina's school bus to arrive from the high school.

But today, unease jumped inside her gut like the kangaroos they'd seen at the zoo in Melbourne. The stranger's appearance had brought back her flight instincts, her survival instincts, her parental instincts.

Tomasine went in search of Sylvie. She checked the schoolyard. She checked Sylvie's classroom and the hall leading to her classroom. She checked the toilets.

She couldn't find her daughter.

Panicked, she hurried to the nearest teacher—a slender blonde who was speaking with another parent. Tomasine interrupted without compunction, grabbing the young woman's forearm and shaking her despite the difference in their size. "My daughter Sylvie. Where is she?"

The teacher's glower faded, replaced by confusion and concern. "I saw her earlier. She must be here." She glanced around the busy schoolyard, her height allowing her to see better than Tomasine. "I don't see her. I'll ask the other teachers." She trotted off, pausing to check with a male teacher before striding into the school.

Meanwhile Tomasine ran to alert Felix. "Felix. I can't find Sylvie. The teacher said she was here but she's not now." Icy fear twisted around her heart at the thought of what the assassins—Joseph's minions—would do to Sylvie. She swallowed, clammy sweat forming on her hands, the rest of her body.

Memories of the massacre flooded her mind. The stench of blood, bright red and vivid. The pained moans from the dying shifters. The screams. Frightened tears flooded her eyes. Sylvie was five. An innocent. None of this was her fault.

Tomasine grasped Felix's arm and dug her fingernails into his flesh. "We have to find her. She's not in her classroom or out here with the other students."

Felix squeezed her, his expression of concern flickering to impassive and strong. "You go and see if the teachers have seen her and I'll organize the parents to search the classrooms and school grounds." He spoke calmly and his quiet strength filtered through Tomasine's stark panic.

Marginally calmer, she retraced her steps, her gaze flickering back and forth, searching each face. Opening every one of her feline senses, she tested the air and listened for any sound that might help locate her daughter. A sob of strained laughter, a trifle hysterical, squeezed free, the calmness of seconds before a mere illusion.

There were so many different scent trails—all shifter. The reason she'd settled in Middlemarch now became a disadvantage. The paths crisscrossed so much that Tomasine couldn't tell which scent trails were fresh from those made earlier this morning. She thought she smelled Sylvie but the track petered out at the edge of a knee-high hedge bordering one of the gardens.

"Mrs. Brooks." The teacher she'd approached earlier appeared from inside the main building. Tomasine couldn't remember her name since she wasn't Sylvie's teacher. She hurried over to the woman, her heart thudding against her ribs so loudly it was a wonder the other woman couldn't hear. "Miss Madison said Sylvie left her classroom with the other students. Since she wasn't on playground duty, Miss Madison has been in her classroom ever since."

"So, where's Sylvie?" Tomasine demanded.

"Don't worry. She must be here somewhere."

"Where?" Tomasine's hands clenched, and she ached to wring the woman's neck. Her daughter was missing, dammit. The school was responsible for Sylvie's wellbeing while she was in attendance.

The teacher took two steps back as if Tomasine might strike her. Instead Tomasine turned away, intending to start checking the classrooms and every single cupboard one by one.

"Tomasine."

Tomasine whirled around on hearing Felix's voice. "Have you found her?"

"No. Gina's bus has arrived. She's looking for Sylvie too. I think we should contact the police."

"The police?" Terror threatened to cut off her breathing. *The police*. God, Sylvie was really gone. Felix slipped his arm around her waist just in time to catch her as her knees buckled. This was her fault. She should have listened to her gut instincts—the ones that shouted to run straightaway instead of letting Felix talk her round.

Her fault.

The words echoed over and over inside her head until she thought she might go mad.

Saber and Leo arrived to help with the search. They and their helpers, along with quite a few non-shifters, searched the area by grid, even areas previously searched.

There was no trace of Sylvie.

Finally three hours later, the searchers met outside the school. Darkness shrouded the familiar landmarks. Security lights flickered on at the school and in the shops and houses farther up the road, sending shards of illumination into the gloom.

Everything in Tomasine felt frozen and the chill kept growing. She shivered, hope surging as each group of searchers returned, then plummeting at the clipped shake of heads.

"Has anyone seen strangers hanging around?" Saber called out over the low, uneasy chatter.

Tomasine held her breath, not wanting the answer to be in the affirmative even though it would give them a starting point in their search.

"Tomasine and I haven't seen anyone," Felix said.

"Me neither," Leo answered.

"I saw a blonde woman not long ago," a man called from the back of the group. "A stranger."

Saber held up a hand to halt the burst of worried discourse. "What did she look like?"

"A slender blonde," the man said. "She wore black."

Tomasine bit back a moan of distress. She leaned into Felix, unable to stop the tremors that racked her body. The assassins she'd seen or come into contact with so far had been men but a woman was capable of the job. Her mouth tightened. She'd killed an assassin and if she could kill, any woman could do the same.

"Where did you see her last? Did anyone else see her?" Felix demanded.

"When I was driving toward the pub," the man said. "About half an hour ago. Maybe forty-five minutes."

"No one else saw her?" Saber asked.

Tomasine scanned the faces, praying for a lead of any kind but not one person spoke up.

"Let's widen our search to include the whole town." Saber directed each group to a different part of the town while some of the locals searched the school again. "Felix, why don't you take Tomasine home?"

Tomasine baulked. "No. I'm staying here to look for my daughter." She shrugged free of Felix's grip and glared at Saber.

She tensed, waiting for him to strike her. A shuddery breath exited when she realized it wasn't going to happen. In Africa, if she'd dared to speak back to her husband or a senior of the clan like that, she would have ended up flat on the ground despite her royal blood.

"God, Saber. You can't make her go home," Felix said in a fierce undertone. "What if it were Emily?"

Saber rubbed a hand through his hair, leaving his dark curls sticking up in all directions. "Sorry. You're right." He squeezed Tomasine's shoulder in silent comfort. "Look after her, Felix."

Felix grabbed her hand and they hurried off to commence searching their allocated area.

"Where's Gina?" Tomasine asked, another streak of fear piercing her chest. She stopped walking to stare at Felix in mute horror. When had she seen Gina last?

"Don't worry. She asked if she could search with her friend. I said yes because they were with Saul, one of my friends. I'd trust him with my life," Felix said. "And Gina's."

The air whooshed from her lungs in relief. She gave a strangled laugh and wiped her clammy palms on the seat of her jeans. "Okay."

Felix caressed her cheek. "Come on. You search this side of the road and I'll do the other. Keep me in sight all the time. Please."

Tomasine nodded, her gaze already searching the shadows cast by three pines. A shadow moved. Her heart stalled before it jump-started again. A horse. A shape moved in her peripheral vision. Hope surged and faded at the soft bleat of a goat. God, Sylvie. She bit back a sob. Her chest hurt. Her eyes prickled and the lump in her throat threatened to choke her. Where was her daughter?

A hoarse male shout sounded several streets over. Tomasine's head jerked up. She froze.

"Tomasine, they've found something," Felix said. "Come on."

She started to run. Outside the school, a group of people gathered. At the sober expressions on their faces she pulled up short, each breath coming in a panicked wheeze. "Sylvie?"

"What is it?" Felix demanded.

The man glanced at her and blurted, "They've found a body."

"Sylvie?" Tomasine staggered, her vision narrowing to a long tunnel. A roar filled her head.

They'd found Sylvie.

A body. They'd found a body.

Sylvie.

Felix's arm came around her trembling shoulders. She heard a whimper, a cry. It took a while to realize the sound came from her.

Saber appeared in front of them. "It's not Sylvie. Tomasine, it's not Sylvie." His tone was fierce as if he knew he had to speak harshly to cut through her panic, her rising self-recriminations.

"Who is it?" Felix asked.

"A stranger. A man. He hasn't been dead long."

"I want to see him," Tomasine said. If it were an assassin, she might recognize him.

"The police are on the scene. They're not shifters. They've cordoned off the area and they're not letting anyone close enough to see a thing," Saber said in an undertone. "We'll have to wait until they move the body. We might be able to have access then."

A phone rang and Tomasine's head jerked up. She heard the low tones of Felix's brother, Leo, as he answered. After a brief conversation, he disconnected.

"Saber, that was Emily." Something in his tone snared Tomasine's attention.

Saber too. "Is something wrong?"

Leo shrugged. "Emily said you should go to Storm in a Teacup right now. She said to take Felix and Tomasine. She wouldn't tell me why, just said she had a problem."

"Sylvie?" Please let it be her daughter. Tomasine glanced at Saber and caught the anxiety flashing across his face. He truly

127

loved his mate. The shifters here in New Zealand didn't operate a rigid clan system like those in Africa. The mates were equal partners. Tomasine sighed in envy for something she'd never had, something she'd never have. She drew herself up and prayed this call related to Sylvie.

"She sounded worried," Leo said. "She told me to make sure it was just family who came."

"Let's go," Saber said. "We'd better make it look casual so we don't attract attention."

They moved off toward Storm in a Teacup. Tomasine glanced at Saber. His face appeared grim as if he carried the weight of the world on his broad back. Felix's expression was similar. Leo as well. It made her want to bawl—the idea that three men, three strangers, would take her into their lives and care for her girls and her without a discernible agenda.

A man stopped them. "Have you found anything?"

"No," Saber answered.

"Tomasine is ready to drop," Felix said, his strong arm curled around her waist supporting his claim. "We're going to Storm in a Teacup for a cup of tea."

"I could do with a drink," the man said with a tired sigh. "Is Emily still open?"

"No," Leo said. "She packed up early today."

"Pity. I might pop home for a quick coffee before I rejoin the search," the man said, with a tired yawn. "This is a worrying business. I have three kids of my own. Don't worry, Mrs. Brooks. We'll find your daughter."

"Thank you," Tomasine whispered hoarsely, once again humbled by the care and concern of the Middlemarch residents.

They continued down the footpath, passing the Middlemarch Bed and Breakfast and the post office. Other groups of people stopped them on the way, and Saber repeated the story they'd told the first man.

By the time they reached Storm in a Teacup at the other end of town, Tomasine's stomach churned huge waves of bile and she thought she might vomit. She wouldn't manage to force down a cup of tea let alone eat.

"Emily said to go around the back," Leo said.

They followed Saber through the gate leading to the outside dining area and to the rear of the café. He knocked on the door.

"Who is it?" Emily demanded.

"Saber."

The door opened and Emily peered out, the anxiety on her face lightening on seeing them. "Oh good. You're all here." She stood aside to let them enter and hurriedly shut the door.

"What is it?" Saber demanded, instantly going to his mate and touching her as if to reassure himself she was okay.

"Um, I think I've found Sylvie," Emily said.

"Sylvie?" Tomasine demanded, whirling to check the kitchen. It was a cruel joke. She couldn't see anything other than pots and pans. A fridge. A freezer. A stainless steel bench workspace. Several boxes of supplies sat on the floor over to her left and a milk crate by the door. It looked as though they'd interrupted Emily in checking off her supplies and putting them away.

A cry sounded, a cross between alarm and panic. It came from behind a pile of boxes.

129

Emily walked across the tiled floor and peeked behind the boxes. "Come out, sweetheart. We won't hurt you."

Another cry sounded along with the noises of stirring. Tomasine's heart pumped out an uneven beat. "Sylvie?"

"I'm not sure, but I think it is Sylvie." As Emily spoke a cat poked its head out of hiding. "At least it had better be Sylvie," she added in a fierce tone. "If this is one of the teenage boys playing a prank, I'll make their lives miserable. And that's a promise."

Leo smirked. "Gave the cat a cuddle, did ya?"

"Shut up," Emily said. "Come on out. Your mama is here."

"Sylvie?" Tomasine's voice croaked and she cleared her throat to try again. "Sylvie."

A small black cat crept from hiding, trembling all over. It was larger than a domestic cat but much smaller than Tomasine when she was in her feline form. The cat had a long black tail and familiar brown eyes.

Tomasine dropped to her knees. "Sylvie, is that you?" The cat let out a pitiful mew. The cry contained confusion along with fear and tore at her heart. She swallowed, frantically wondering what to do. Her daughter was years too young to shift.

Felix crouched at her side and ran a calming hand down Sylvie's back. "Can you change back, sweetheart?"

"I didn't think feline shifters could shift until they were around sixteen. Gina's age," Emily said.

"That's normal. None of us changed for the first time until we were that age," Saber said. "But it's obvious Sylvie is cleverer than all of us." He crossed the tiled floor to crouch beside Felix.

Tomasine noticed her daughter was calmer due to Felix's gentle handling and her trembling had ceased.

"Have you talked to Sylvie about the change?" Felix murmured. He scratched Sylvie behind the ears and a purr erupted.

"I...no." Tomasine flinched. What sort of a mother was she? Dragging her child and Gina all over the world, barely managing to survive life on the run. With all the other stuff going on, she hadn't even prepared Sylvie for the part of her life that was a time of celebration. "She's five. I thought I had loads of time."

Felix paused in his stroking of Sylvie. "Tomasine, don't beat yourself up. Our uncle who looked after us after our parents died never spoke a word of the change until we turned twelve."

"I've talked to Gina."

"Of course you have," Saber said. "You're a good mother. No one could have foreseen Sylvie changing at this early age."

His soothing words failed to comfort her. "How do I explain to her how to change back? You can dress it up all you want but the change hurts."

"What happened to her shredded clothes? Why didn't we find them?" Felix asked. "And why did she come here instead of going home? Or waiting for you. She would have known you'd be waiting to collect her after school."

Felix was right. They should have found her clothes and school bag yet they hadn't. Fear escalated in Tomasine again. Someone knew Sylvie was a shifter. Her hands shook violently and she must have made a sound.

"Emily, can you make a cup of tea?" Felix asked. "Tomasine. Let me help Sylvie. She's used to me and you know I wouldn't do anything to cause her unnecessary pain."

Tomasine lifted her chin to glare at Felix. "But—"

One look at Felix's calm face and she conceded. Her shoulders drooped and her attitude dispersed. Her entire body was wound tight with tension and her daughter recognized this. The poor kid probably feared anger and lectures. None of this was her fault. If things were different...

"All right." She attempted a soothing voice for Sylvie but it didn't quite come off, sounding angry instead. Sylvie whimpered and squeezed closer to Felix. It felt like a slap across the face. She inhaled, trying to calm herself as much as her daughter. Slowly, she stood and moved away, stepping across the tiled floor toward the chest freezer.

Emily walked over to Tomasine and pressed her onto a wooden chair on the other side of the large double door fridge. "Trust Felix. He's a good man."

But Sylvie was her daughter. Tomasine remained silent, her gaze on the small black leopard.

Emily bustled around making tea while Leo picked up an empty green milk crate, sat it on its end, positioning it beside her to use as a seat. He reached over and patted her hand. Tomasine stared at her daughter as Sylvie concentrated on Felix, listening to his hushed voice. She tried to imagine Bernard or any of his family giving the same comfort and help. It would never happen. A snort escaped, loud enough for Leo to look askance.

"Sorry," she muttered, her gaze intent on her daughter. Bernard had hated any perceived weakness, probably because

132

her deceased husband bore the gene himself and tried to overcompensate.

Felix smoothed his hand along Sylvie's back. "Concentrate for me, Sylvie. Remember what I used to do when I was a little boy. I imagined a black cat. I'd draw a head and add the body and a long, swishing tail inside my mind." He paused, feeling the child's trepidation and shock. Understandable given the circumstances. "That would make the change start."

Sylvie stopped purring and quivered again. A wave of tenderness swept him. He loved this little kitten as much as he loved Tomasine.

Loved.

The thought gave him pause but it was a great feeling. The responsibility didn't scare him.

"Remember what you looked like this morning?" he said. "I want you to draw your clothes inside your head."

Sylvie looked at him with her big brown eyes. They narrowed fractionally and her whiskers twitched in a feline frown. She needed more help.

"Then once you've drawn your clothes and added your shoes, I want you to think about your reflection when you look in a mirror to brush your hair. Can you do that?"

Sylvie nodded and her eyes closed. Her nose wrinkled in a cute manner that made him grin. He glanced up to catch Saber's silent approval.

At the sound of a phone Felix tensed, but to his relief Sylvie kept concentrating. He heard Tomasine's voice croak before his brother Leo plucked the cell phone from her fumbling fingers and answered it for her.

Felix continued to speak to Sylvie in a soothing voice, repeating his instructions calmly even though worry pulsed inside him. What if he couldn't talk Sylvie back to human form? He'd heard of it happening before. Hell, he understood her fear. Transforming the first time was traumatic enough. He remembered it well. But on the plus side, the euphoric feeling of running, being at one with the elements—there was nothing like it. Sylvie hadn't experienced that yet but she would as soon as he could make arrangements.

"Can you see yourself in your mind?"

Sylvie grunted and rubbed her head against his knee.

"Good girl. Now I want you to make a magic wish. Keep your eyes closed and wish hard that you looked like that right now. Can you do that for me?"

A tremor rippled through her slight frame. Her eyes popped open. They were full of dread. He stroked her neck and after studying him intently, she closed her eyes. A few tense seconds passed and he started to worry. He glanced at Saber but his older brother gave a slight shake of his head and an encouraging smile. Felix studied Sylvie, willing the familiar shimmer around her body to start. When he'd almost given up, the tension in the kitchen so strong Emily could have served it up in slices and sold it in the café, a faint glow formed around Sylvie. The glow increased and Felix's shoulders relaxed. Past the point of no return.

Sylvie whimpered, her limbs thrashing, but it was too late for her to stop. As Felix watched, her fur disappeared turning to flesh.

"Is there something she can wear?" Felix asked.

Leo whipped off his shirt and handed it to Felix. "Use this. I have a spare one in the ute."

By the time he'd taken the dark blue shirt from Leo, Sylvie stood before him, tears streaming down her face. He whisked the shirt over her head, gave her a quick hug. Tomasine elbowed him aside, throwing herself at Sylvie and enveloping her in a fierce embrace.

"Tomasine," Felix said, after a long moment. "We need to discover what happened to Sylvie. I know she's been through a lot but we have to learn about her clothes and bag."

Tomasine loosened her grip but didn't release her. "Can...can you tell us what happened? It's very important."

"I wasn't feeling well," Sylvie said in a whisper.

Felix crouched again and smiled in encouragement even though he ached to gather up his new family and take them home where he knew they'd be safe. "So what did you do?"

"I went outside. I felt sick so I hid behind a tree." Her bottom lip quivered. "I didn't want the other children to see me and laugh."

Felix nodded. "Then what happened?"

"My bones hurt." Big tears formed in her eyes, making Felix swallow. He hated crying women since they brought feelings of helplessness to the surface and he never knew what to do. It seemed tiny girls had the same effect.

SHELLEY MUNRO

"What did you do then?" Tomasine smoothed her daughter's hair from her face and Saber produced a hanky.

"I turned into a kitty. The lady found me and told me to come here to Emily."

"What lady?" Tomasine demanded.

"Tell us what the lady looked like," Felix said.

"She was pretty."

Felix glanced up in frustration and intercepted his brothers' smirks. They brought an answering grin to his face. Better laughing than crying.

A tap sounded on the door. "That will be Gina," Leo said. "I told her we were here."

"What was the lady wearing?" Tomasine asked. "What color was her hair?"

"She had white hair," Sylvie said. "And black clothes."

"The blonde lady," Tomasine said in a hoarse voice.

"Sylvie. You okay?" Gina winked at Sylvie before scanning the room. When her gaze reached Leo, her eyes rounded. "Oh nice."

"Gina, you're sixteen," Leo said sharply. "You are not meant to ogle men and especially not me."

A soft blush swept her chubby cheeks but she stood her ground. "Why not?"

"Yeah, Leo," Emily said. "Why not? I mean you're so pretty to look at."

"You." Saber glared at his mate. "Eyes off my brother."

"Spoilsport," Emily whispered, her eyes twinkling with naughtiness.

"Tell us about the lady," Felix said.

"The lady was nice. She picked up my clothes and bag for me." Sylvie frowned. "I couldn't do it. No hands." She held out her hands and wriggled her fingers, her expression one of relief. "I have hands now."

"I heard about the blonde woman," Gina said. "No one's seen her recently. But no one's looking for her either. They're all in an uproar. The body has disappeared."

Chapter 8

Lost Bodies and Unease

"**D**isappeared?" Tomasine's nose wrinkled in an astonished frown. How could a body disappear?

"Yeah. The cops did a crime scene investigation. The dead male was loaded in an ambulance to take to Dunedin but someone stopped it en route and stole the body. Weird, huh?" Gina's glance strayed to Leo and lingered for a long moment before she sighed and looked back to Felix. "I heard he didn't have any identification. They don't know who he was."

Tomasine didn't like the sound of that one bit. It solidified one thing in her mind. She must leave. It was too late now. Sylvie needed a good night's rest. They'd leave tomorrow morning. "I need to get Sylvie to bed."

"I'll drive you," Felix said.

"You almost done, Emily?" Saber asked. "I want to learn more about this mysterious disappearing body."

The blonde woman worried her. Even though Sylvie insisted the woman had helped, Tomasine didn't like knowing she was out there—unpredictable. An unknown quantity.

Surprises were bad.

Tomasine gripped her daughter's hand so hard Sylvie yelped in protest. She loosened her grasp. "Sorry."

"Let me carry her to the vehicle," Felix said, easing her aside and scooping Sylvie into his arms. "Coming, Gina? You're staying at the homestead for a while."

"Really?" Gina beamed at Leo. "Cool. I'll drive out with Leo."

Felix heard his younger brother mutter under his breath but Leo didn't snap at the teenager.

"I'm leaving now," Leo said, leaping off the milk crate. He replaced it in the corner where he'd found it with a distinct thump and Felix bit back a smirk. It was good to see his brother maneuvered with such ease. It took a master to beat Leo.

An hour later, Tomasine lingered in the girls' bedroom, trying to quash the dread that stalked her mind. She didn't like coincidences. The strange woman, the disappearing body—instinct told her they were both something to do with her. Damn Joseph. Why couldn't he accept she wanted nothing to do with the clan? It wasn't as if there were any true clan members left to rule. Only his friends and family, and of course, the wealth and resources owned by the clan—the gemstone quarry, the mineral resources and the business interests still in the clan name.

He was welcome to everything.

The bedroom door opened. Her head jerked up and she only relaxed when she recognized Emily.

"Is Sylvie asleep?" she asked.

Tomasine nodded before realizing that Emily's eyesight wasn't as good as hers. "Yes, she's asleep."

"Dinner's ready," Emily said. "We'll leave the door open so we can hear if she wakes. The boys have checked outside several times. She's safe here. We're not going to let anything happen to Sylvie or you and Gina."

"I'm not hungry." Emotion stopped her from saying anything else. She swallowed and attempted a stoic appearance. Now wasn't the time to fall apart.

"You need to eat to keep up your strength," Emily said in a firm voice. "It's safe to eat since I cooked tonight instead of one of the boys. Besides, if you don't come out, Felix will arrive to hassle you next."

Despite the terror stalking her thoughts, a sliver of longing zapped through Tomasine. Felix was a male she could care for—if she let herself. She blinked away the tears that formed without warning and forced a smile. *Tomorrow.* Tomorrow, they'd leave.

"Too late. I'm already here." Felix's deep voice came from the doorway. "You need to eat. You can't help Sylvie if you get sick."

"All right." The truth in his words persuaded her to change her mind. That and the fact she wanted to store memories of Felix's face, his smile and the timbre of his voice to pull out later when she struggled alone.

The bittersweet meal passed too quickly. They had a heated discussion about music. Leo liked New Zealand music and was passionate in defending the homegrown bands and solo artists while Gina adored the latest English boy band. Tomasine approved of the way Leo turned aside Gina's flirtation and obvious puppy love but still treated her as an adult.

She stood once everyone finished eating. "I'll do the dishes."

"No, stay there. It's Saber and Leo's turn tonight," Emily said.

"Don't argue. You'll get your turn soon enough," Saber said. "Emily has us organized."

Guilt rose then. The Mitchell family was welcoming and accepting, and she intended to sneak off like a thief in the middle of a night. With an assassin lurking around Middlemarch, everyone was in danger. If she and the girls left, everyone would be safe.

"I'll check on Sylvie," she said. "Gina, have you done your homework?"

Gina rolled her eyes. "Aw, Tom."

"Better do it quick, Gina, or else Emily won't let you use the Play Station," Felix teased. "She's very bossy."

Tomasine slid from the room in the midst of Emily's strident complaint about smart-mouthed brothers-in-law. A tear spilled down her face while her chest tightened so much she had trouble drawing a breath. They were close. The good-natured insults and bickering brought home how lonely it was on the run and how draining it was looking over her shoulder and wondering where the next assassin would leap from.

Sylvie was sound asleep with the top of her head showing above the blankets as per normal.

"Is she okay?"

Tomasine started when Felix spoke from behind her. It took long seconds for her pulse rate to settle after his hands closed over her tense shoulders. "She's fine. I should have noticed she wasn't well." Guilt whispered in her ear again. She'd been preoccupied with Felix and the way he made her feel. What kind of mother was she?

"Come on." Felix tugged her from Sylvie's room. "You need to sleep. You won't be much good to Sylvie if you're tired."

Felix couldn't have picked a better way to persuade her to leave her daughter's room. When they left Middlemarch tomorrow, she'd need her wits about her.

He led her into his bedroom and closed the door. Immediately, the tension between them lurched upward. He smiled, a slow, sexy curve of lips. She saw it clearly despite the absence of full light. "You need sleep," he said. "I want to hold you."

Yes. Tomasine wanted that too, but she also needed more memories. Since she knew Sylvie was safe, this was the time to grab memories, something for herself. "I'm not that tired," she purred.

His smile turned to a full-out grin. "I was hoping you'd say that."

Amazing. If she'd said no, he would have accepted her response without argument. Felix would have just held her.

"I want you." Tomasine held his gaze as she stepped away from him. Without haste, her hands went to the buttons on her cotton shirt. She unfastened them one by one, peeling the material from her body in a seductive manner. She watched the green of his eyes darken. His broad chest rose and fell and his grin faded. Intently he watched her every action. Tomasine let the shirt fall to the floor. She unbuckled her leather belt and unfastened her jeans. With a sassy wiggle of hips, she shimmied from the tight denim and kicked them aside. Hmm, there was no sexy way to remove cotton socks. Tomasine planted her butt on the bed and did her best to look tempting. She puckered her lips in a kiss and leaned back, lifting one leg at the same time.

Felix stepped close and rolled the cotton sock down her ankle and off her foot. He tossed it aside. Grinning, she extended her other foot toward him. He repeated the competent move, his innocent touch sending sensual messages zipping straight to her sex.

"What's next?" Eyes gleaming with interest, Felix moved back, stepping into a shaft of moonlight. He looked so good in his tight faded jeans and plain dark green T-shirt that her chest hurt, and the way he caressed her with his gaze made her feel special. Desired. Sexy. Definitely aroused.

Tomasine stood and sashayed toward him. "It wouldn't hurt if you showed a little skin." She slipped one hand beneath the hem of his T-shirt and explored the warm flesh beneath. The muscular stomach quivered as she smoothed her palm across it but other than that, he didn't react. It became a challenge, a fervent need to make him lose control.

Felix would never hurt her—she knew it with every survival instinct she possessed. She smoothed her hand upward across his ribs and a pectoral muscle. Nimble fingers sought a flat masculine nipple. She'd show him control. But first...

"Lift your arms."

His eyes narrowed the tiniest fraction. If she hadn't watched closely, she would have missed the reaction. Standing on tiptoes, she lifted the T-shirt over his head, struggling to complete the operation because of his height. Finally, Felix ripped the T-shirt off and chucked it on the bed.

"What's next?"

Tomasine flicked out her tongue and he followed the slick move with avid interest. His clean scent filled her every breath while the moonlight sent dappled patterns across his skin. Desire stirred, threatening to flare out of control, but she tamped it down, determined to go slow and make special memories. Her hand glided across the hard contours of his chest, the dense muscles and tanned skin garnered from physical work on the farm. With her fingernails, she flicked a masculine nipple. Under her fascinated gaze, it tightened to a hard nub. She lowered her head and licked the small disc. A salty tang sprang across her taste buds. Tomasine repeated the move and bit down. Felix grunted but his hand came up to hold her in place, his fingers twining through her long hair, silently signaling her to continue.

Tomasine alternately nipped and licked to soothe the sting. Felix remained silent but his hands moved from her hair, sliding down her back to cup her butt. He drew her closer, pulling her against his erection, letting her know how much he wanted her and liked what she was doing to him. Yearning kicked her in the belly while juices gathered at the intimate juncture of her thighs.

It was difficult to go slow with urgency thundering inside her. Her mind greedily snapped up experiences, the harsh gasp whenever she bit him, the pleasuring stroke of his fingers and the sweet agony that thrummed to life in her.

She needed him naked.

With rapid, jerky moves she struggled with the button on his jeans and the zipper.

"Careful, sweetheart. I don't want you to maim me at this stage of proceedings." The lazy humor in his voice brought a surge of emotion in Tomasine. This man—he was perfect in every way. Sadly it was the wrong time. Wrong place. Regrets assailed her but she pushed them aside to concentrate on tonight.

The present.

Tomasine maneuvered the denim and boxers away from his erection and pushed them down his legs. He lifted one leg after the other so she could remove his clothes and finally he stood before her wearing nothing but a smile. No socks for Felix.

"You're stunning to look at," she murmured, sitting back on her heels to admire the scenery. His chest was broad and almost hair free, his stomach was flat and muscular while his hips were lean. She stood and circled him, scrutinizing his body at the same time. And his butt—well that was truly magnificent. She paused to appreciate the view and bent to take a bite.

Felix winced and then sniggered. He pulled from her touch and turned to study her, his green eyes glowing with laughter. "I've been told my butt was fine but I didn't realize it was that tempting."

"I wanted to taste. Um, nice view from the front too."

Grinning, he curled his hand around his erect cock and pumped it to greater prominence. "Whatcha gonna do with me now?" His voice contained a smoky quality that pushed every one of her buttons.

Carnal fantasies flooded her mind. Oh there were lots of things she wanted to do to his sexy body. Sheer physical perfection and for tonight, all hers. Heat stabbed straight to her pussy, and her tongue slipped out again to soothe dry lips.

"I'm going to explore your body with close attention to detail," she whispered, circling his form again. "I'm going to kiss you, straddle your hips and ride you until we both explode."

"Sounds good." Felix paused and caught her eye. "As long as you take your lingerie off first."

Tomasine rolled her eyes. "That is a given."

"All right." Felix folded his arms against his chest. "Time starts now."

"Uh-uh." She restrained her laughter and shook her head. "My game. We'll take things at my speed."

"I'm bigger and stronger than you."

"But you're not a bully," she countered.

Bernard, her husband, had been a bully so she knew the difference. In hindsight, she realized the man had taken her in, played her like a master, fueling her need for family because he'd wanted control of the clan. "You won't lift a finger to hurt me."

"I could torture you—tie you up and pleasure you until you can't take any more."

She imagined the scenario before letting out a long pent-up breath. "Yes please."

"Are you sure you want control right now? I'm happy to take over." He closed the distance between them while he was speaking.

Tomasine held her hands up in front of her in a stop signal, laughing the whole time. "Oh no you don't." She backed until the bed stopped farther retreat.

"Now I have you right where I want you." His brows rose and fell and he twirled an imaginary moustache. Felix stood so close she felt the heat from his naked form and his cock brushed her lower belly. It left a damp mark on her skin and brought an answering flood of arousal to her pussy.

Time to wrest back control. "Do you have a condom?"

"Yeah." He dipped his head to steal a kiss. His lips moved against hers briefly before he nibbled her bottom lip. Felix pulled away so they were no longer touching. "The drawer on the left-hand side. I hope there's enough. I'd hate to beg for more from Leo."

Heat crowded her face at the thought. They hadn't used a condom earlier. She hoped there were no repercussions. It wasn't like her to take risks like that. "On the bed, Felix. Now." She barked out the command to counteract her thoughts. Too late to worry now but she wouldn't repeat the mistake.

Felix sat on the edge of the bed and rolled into the middle. With his hands tucked under his head, he appeared at ease. The tic of a pulse point in his jaw hinted at his true emotions. He was having trouble holding back but was doing his best to cooperate.

Trustworthy.

Loyal.

A hunk.

She could add loving to her list as well. Felix would make an excellent mate. Too bad things weren't different.

"Are you going to do anything soon?" he asked, his voice husky with need and a trace of impatience.

"I want to make this good for both of us." She stroked one corded thigh with a butterfly touch. Trailing her fingers upward, she brushed his testicles. They were swollen and moved under the skin, reminding her of waves in the sea. Biting her lip to stem a bark of laughter, she leaned closer and puffed warm air over them. He widened his legs, giving her room to move between. She took advantage, edging closer. Dipping her head, Tomasine blew another stream of hot air over his balls, pursing her lips so she was almost touching him. He shivered, and when she glanced up, his eyes were squeezed shut, his muscles tense as if he were waiting for more.

So, she'd give him more. She grinned, liking the freedom to explore and experiment. She'd definitely give him more. After one more round of blowing, she changed tack and nuzzled his balls, tracing the seam between them with a lazy sweep of her tongue.

His hand tangled in her hair. At first she thought he was protesting but he let out a soft purr and massaged her scalp with a light touch. She continued her explorations, playfully licking, savoring the scent of his arousal and the salty taste of his skin. The contented purring continued and whenever she glanced up, his eyes were closed and his mouth curved in a smile.

Tomasine licked his testicles all over with tiny licks, probing between with the tip of her tongue. She nibbled with her lips, taking care to keep her lengthening canines away. With her lips and tongue she maneuvered one into her mouth, the balls hardening with her teasing. A smile played across her lips and

148

she hummed with enjoyment. The realization she held power over him and could hurt him if she desired brought deeper understanding.

With Bernard, her inexperience had worked against her. The politics and intrigue amongst the powerful males in the tribe seeking to gain her hand and the crown had made her miss the simple pleasures of just being with a male, loving him. Felix had given a part of herself back she hadn't known was missing.

With enthusiasm, she continued her sensual investigation. Tomasine licked a taut ball and strayed to the root of his erect penis. The massaging hand at her head ceased all movement when she trailed her tongue along the underside of his cock, upward until she almost touched his tip. He shuddered.

"Again. God, Tomasine, please do that again. The roughness of your tongue feels so damn good."

Tomasine lifted her head and she saw his eyes were open, an intense green and swirling with heat and passion. "And if I refuse?"

"I won't use my tongue on you," he whispered. "You know how good it feels—the rough texture tugging at sensitive flesh."

Oh yeah. She knew.

Tomasine repeated the move for him and swirled her tongue around the broad head. A bead of pre-cum formed at the slit and she cleaned it away with a flutter of her tongue.

"Tomasine. Woman, I love you."

She froze for an instant, her warm breath feathering across the head of his cock. He groaned again, not noticing her reaction. Damn. He couldn't love her. She didn't want to hurt him, but she had to leave. Oh he might be angry but she'd thought this was a fling. A little light entertainment to while away the hours. Despite his insistence they were mates, she hadn't truly believed or dared to hope. She didn't believe in luck.

Tomasine teased him with her tongue and used the fingers of one hand to massage his perineum with firm, walking steps. She pressed before continuing the move again and again with her fingers while she battled her conscience. When it came down to it, there was one option. And she'd seize it.

Safety.

Forcing her thoughts back to Felix, she took him into her mouth, swirling her tongue across the sensitive head of his shaft. She brushed her finger across his puckered rosette and dipped it inside, timing her move to coincide with the brush of her tongue.

"That feels good." Felix punctuated his words with a loud purr.

His words, his reactions made her feel powerful. Dominant. It made her feel as though she were equal instead of a submissive mate. Tomasine licked away the seminal fluid that formed on the head and gently pushed her finger into his anus far enough to rub his prostate gland. Felix groaned and thrust his cock deeper into her mouth.

Tomasine was worried about hurting him with her teeth but she did her best, sucking and licking his sensitive tip while continuing a slow stimulation of his gland. He thrust again, withdrawing from her mouth a fraction to thrust again. His large frame trembled. His purrs transformed to groans.

Tomasine pressed down on his prostate and he tensed, his cock seeming to swell even larger. She sucked, her cheeks hollowing. A dark sound rippled from deep in his throat and he came with a sudden rush. She swallowed rapidly, holding his cock in her mouth until he quietened. After one final lick, she pulled back to see him watching her. Heat shimmered in his eyes, promising all sorts of things she wasn't sure she wanted—not when it would lead to heartache.

She bent her head and pressed a kiss to his hipbone. Gradually, she worked up his body, feathering kisses over muscled contours, nibbling at his pectoral muscle and letting him feel the bite of her canines. A drop of blood beaded and she lazily licked it away.

He growled deep in his throat, making her smile. His cock jerked against her hip, surprising Tomasine. His recuperative powers were astonishingly quick. *Lucky her*.

And as if to underline her thoughts, he said, "Come here, sweetheart. That hasn't even dented my need."

"Condom first." Blistering waves of arousal consumed Tomasine and all she'd done was pleasure him. Her panties were damp with her juices while her bra was an encumbrance.

She craved a night to remember. She needed this desperately and the inherent hope the memory held—that one day she might have a normal life. This last night with Felix would help in the dark days to come, the frightening days alone when she relied on her own skill and cunning.

He licked his lips. "In the drawer."

She wrenched open the drawer he'd indicated and grabbed a condom. Turning back to him, she ripped open the foil packet and let her gaze crawl across his swollen cock. It pointed toward his belly, the head broad and flared.

She swallowed, remembering what he felt like stretching her channel and pushing impossibly deep. And her climax—the way it ripped through her body sometimes with an explosive force while other times it was slow and lazy and went on for long seconds of unbearable tension. She tugged off her panties and bra and flung them aside. Her pussy fluttered, the pressure climbing inside her. Impatient now, she pushed him back until he lay flat on the mattress and straddled his body.

Felix stared up at her, his handsome face tight with the same wanting, the same desire that thrummed through her. Holding his gaze, she guided his cock to her wet center and with a twist—a hip gyration—she impaled herself. Her inner muscles clung lovingly to the flare of his cock. Slowly, she sank downward, watching his face the entire time. His gaze was a phantom caress, every part of her prickling as if he'd brushed his fingers over her with a delicate touch. When she was fully seated, she paused, swaying a fraction to savor the way he felt inside her.

Her nostrils flared as she inhaled to store scents while her gaze danced across his face, his hair, his chest, taking in the small details she'd need for later. She leaned closer to trace his sensual lips with her tongue. When he opened his mouth, she took advantage, letting her tongue surge inside while she kissed him. The kiss started almost chastely before it turned carnal and desperate. Lips that had sipped now demanded. The sleek thrust of his tongue against hers drove her toward desperation. A raw and guttural groan ripped from her throat and she pulled back, staring at him, her heart pumping so hard it felt as though it might bounce from her chest.

Without breaking their gazes, she started to ride him. Swaying and rolling her hips, she set a rhythm entirely to her satisfaction. It felt amazing—the pull of delicate inner muscles, the wet sound of arousal as their bodies slid against each other.

Amazing.

Magical.

Memorable.

The clawing tension in her pussy intensified with each upward stroke of his cock, each downward slide. Her heart continued to misbehave, lurching painfully when she noted the expression in his eyes—the passion underlined with caring.

With love.

Tomasine shied from the thought and squeezed her eyes shut. It was easier to concentrate on greedily snatching memories when she didn't have to face Felix, knowing she would hurt him. Hurt herself. Tipping her head back, she quickened her pace. A moan fell from her lips as an intense burst of heat flickered through her. Harder. Faster. She swiveled in order to hit her clit at the perfect angle.

He grasped her hips, fingers branding her flesh as he urged her to speed. A familiar low pressure gathered. Close but not close enough. She cupped her breasts and pinched one nipple. The small pain echoed in her sex.

"Touch yourself," Felix murmured.

Her eyes flicked open to see the intent expression on his face, the tinge of color in his cheekbones. She hesitated, rising and falling again on his cock. A tremble racked her as she struggled toward completion. Part of her was greedy while another part desperately wanted to draw out her pleasure.

"Go on. I want to watch."

"Pervert." A grin flashed seconds before her hands smoothed down her rib cage. She rode his cock, sinking downward. At the same time, she parted moist folds with her fingers. She made a teasing pass over her swollen clit.

"Ohhh," she whispered.

"Feel good?"

She swayed and repeated the move. "Oh yes. Yeah, it's wonderful." Every nerve ending seemed to vibrate. Time stood still for an instant as she rose then slid down his erection. She delved between her legs, plucking and stroking her engorged and needy clitoris. Tomasine tried to stretch it out. She really did, but the wanting, the needing, grew to bursting. The pleasure built to a plateau where she hovered for an instant longer.

"Now," Felix said insistently, his hands gripping her hips as he drove up into her pussy. "Now."

Without warning she exploded, convulsing around his cock. She gasped when he slammed upward into her pussy again. A hoarse cry escaped his clenched jaw and he froze, locked deep inside her body. His cock jerked while she luxuriated in the myriad aftershocks.

"Tomasine." Felix's eyes squeezed tight for a brief second before he sought her gaze. He stared deep into her eyes, expressing silent emotions that frightened her. They made her yearn for more, more than she could ever have.

Chapter 9

Time to Say Goodbye

Tomasine woke with the early morning sun streaming through the window. Alone, the dip in the pillow at her side the sole indication of Felix's presence during the night. She stood, wincing at the pull of tight muscles from their run yesterday. They'd made love several times during the night and she bore lingering aches from that too. While she had no regrets, she didn't have time for a long soak in the bath. Not today. She dressed rapidly, collected the few possessions she'd unpacked the previous night and placed them in her bag. After zipping it shut, she did one final scan before going to check on Sylvie and Gina.

Sylvie's bedroom was empty. For an instant she panicked then she heard laughter coming from the other end of the house—girlish laughter along with a husky male chuckle. Two males, she saw when she burst into the kitchen.

Felix sauntered toward her, a gleam in his eyes. From the corner of her eye she caught Leo's smirk. Hopefully Gina wasn't watching. If ever a smirk was X-rated, it was that one.

Tomasine concentrated on Felix while attempting to subdue the dull pain and sorrow clutching her chest. She must leave for all their sakes, but it had never been this difficult before.

Despite the audience, Felix placed his hands on her shoulders and kissed her thoroughly and without haste. "Morning, sweetheart," he whispered when he raised his head. He cupped her cheek, the tenderness in his gaze turning the blunt knife in her heart.

"Do you like kissing my mama?" Sylvie asked.

They both looked down at Sylvie who was cocking her head to one side. She reminded Tomasine of an inquisitive bird.

"Yes." Felix glanced at Tomasine, one eyebrow raised as if he expected her to protest. There was no point making an issue of it when she intended to leave. She wanted to blurt it out now but instead she smiled. The type of smile she mourned whenever she saw it from Gina, yet she couldn't raise the energy to sell happiness when she felt so rotten inside.

"Coffee?" Leo asked.

"I'll get it," Gina said, moving across the kitchen to retrieve a mug from one of the cupboards, at home with the Mitchells.

"Anyone for toast?" Emily asked as she breezed into the kitchen followed by Saber.

"Or cereal?" Saber added, opening a cupboard to extract a box of cornflakes.

"I think there's still fruit in the fridge." Emily grinned as if she expected a reaction.

Felix snorted. "Rabbit food. Where's the meat, woman?"

"I think we're facing a losing battle," Leo said, giving his sister-in-law a hard stare.

Emily giggled and placed a bowl of stewed apples in front of him.

Tomasine forced aside a pang of regret at the people she was leaving behind. Good people. It was safer if they left.

She *was* doing the right thing.

Breakfast was a noisy meal, pretty much the same as dinner the previous night. Tomasine tried to participate and knew she wasn't doing a good job upon intercepting a worried glance from Felix who was sitting opposite her. Feeling a hypocrite and hating herself for it, she puckered her lips and blew him a kiss across the table. At least it made him smile. She shouldn't lead him on when they had no future together. She shouldn't but she would because it meant survival.

For not the first time in her life, she cursed the fates. Being royal meant responsibilities—ones she'd failed. None of her forebears had botched up as she had by mistaking charm and good looks for love. She refused to put Sylvie—next in line—through the same torment she'd gone through with Bernard. No, an anonymous life was best if she wanted her daughter to grow into a well-adjusted shifter. Once she was older and able to understand, she would tell Sylvie of her royal heritage but meanwhile she wanted to give her daughter as natural an upbringing as possible.

"What time do you need to be at the bus?" Saber asked. "I can drop the girls off when I take Emily in to the café."

"I thought they could stay home today. I know it's fine but after yesterday..." Tomasine shrugged, trailing off and hoping her body language would tell the story she wanted to broadcast. "I might have a shower," she added, desperate to escape the people—her friends—before she broke down and cried.

Emily stood. "I'll show you where the clean towels are kept."

"Thanks." She followed Emily from the room without looking back. It was that or burst out bawling.

Felix walked into the girls' room while Tomasine was packing. She'd already told Gina and for the first time ever, the girl had pitched a full-scale fit and stormed off to see Leo. No doubt Leo had told Felix.

"Gina said you're leaving." Felix leaned against the doorjamb but it was a pose. Every muscle looked tense, coiled and ready to spring.

She aimed for nonchalance even though inside she was a writhing mass of nerves. Her gaze flickered across his face and in an act of cowardice darted away to study her feet. "It's not safe for any of us. I have to leave while I can. Believe me, you don't want the people hunting me to arrive in Middlemarch. They'll shoot first and ask questions later."

"Who is hunting you? Why?" Although his voice was slow and lazy, she didn't make the mistake of missing his anger, not when it shouted from every line of his tense frame.

"I can't tell you." She'd decided never to mention her royal status again and most definitely not to a shifter. Any male who mated with her had instant power because she was queen of her clan. The female line in her family held the power even though the male who eventually mated with them often took over the rule for their lifetime. In Bernard's case, it had gone to his head and a good portion of the clan had paid with their lives including Bernard. Now Joseph sought to rule. He wanted absolute rule, and the way to secure that power was to mate with her or prove her dead. As next of kin to Bernard and since all her family were dead, he could exert a claim. The power would become absolute if he found proof of Tomasine's and Sylvie's deaths, hence the assassins on their trail.

"Won't tell me." Felix's fists clenched, his glare practically drilling a hole in her face. "I love you. Doesn't that mean anything to you?"

Finally she found the courage to lift her gaze. "My husband told me he loved me. He didn't."

His jaw worked. Tomasine stepped back, putting more space between them. The fact didn't escape him. He snorted. "Don't insult me any more than you have already."

She closed her eyes, acknowledging the hit. In her heart she knew Felix would never hurt her. She couldn't say for sure how she knew—she just did.

"I have to go. I can't risk my children's lives and I'd hate to put any of you in danger. We don't know the identity of the dead man or the mystery blonde woman. My gut is screaming it's something to do with me. I've learned to trust my instincts and they're screeching at me to run."

"Where will you go?"

"The city is the best place. It's busy and easy to hide amongst the crowds, the smells."

"What about Sylvie?"

Bewildered, Tomasine stared. "What do you mean? What about Sylvie?"

"Have you forgotten she went through her first change yesterday? She's too young to control the urge to shift. What are you going to do if she changes in the middle of the city? Besides," he added. "I don't like cities. I tried to live in the city with my girlfriend Alicia." He scowled at the memory. "It felt as if I were smothered alive. I don't want to do it again—"

"I'm not asking you to," Tomasine snapped.

"I'd do it for you," he stated. Even though he'd prefer not to go through that hell again, he hated the thought of living apart from her even more.

Felix held his breath while he waited for her response. God, he couldn't lose her, not now. It would kill him if she walked away. His mouth firmed and he came to a decision. She wasn't going anywhere without him. He should have followed the siren demand that had whispered to him ever since the collision outside the post office. He should have claimed her, taking away her options. Felix sighed. Shit, who was he kidding? As much as he loved her, he wanted her to choose him. He wanted to feel like a winner, make the mating a celebration of mutual love.

"I'll manage somehow," she said, although her face had paled so much he noticed she had a few freckles on the bridge of her nose. He hated knowing he was partially responsible for that fear.

Felix took her hand and dragged her unresisting form down the passage to the kitchen. Saber, Emily, Leo and Gina were sitting around the table with mugs of coffee in front of them while books and crayons surrounded Sylvie.

"Tomasine is insisting on leaving. Talk to her. She won't listen to me." Felix didn't hold back on his frustration. It colored his words and left an awkward silence before everyone started talking at once. It was a case of five against one with the argument going around in circles. Endless circles that made Felix want to put his fist through the nearest wall.

"We could go and stay with Saul's uncle. His station is secluded and safe. We could help with the farm work," he said.

"No."

"What's wrong with staying with Saul's uncle? We've known Saul since we were Sylvie's age. I'd trust him and his family with my life."

"Are you sure?" Tomasine demanded. "Because that's what you'd be doing."

A strident knock on the front door broke their deadlock. Felix watched Tomasine's head jerk in the direction of the summons. Probably glad of the respite since his arguments were so persuasive. At least he thought they were. They made sense, dammit. Surely she'd change her mind about leaving. Tomasine couldn't leave. He wouldn't let her out of his sight or the girls.

Tomasine scowled at them, one by one. "I don't think it's a good idea to hide so close to Middlemarch."

"But the security is excellent. Saul's uncle and all his workers are shifters. It's difficult to sneak up on the farm. I know because we tried a few times when we were younger," Leo said.

The impatient hammering came again.

"I'll get it," Emily said.

"No, wait here. I'll go," Saber said. "It's not a local. They'd know to come to the other door."

Immediately tension rose in Tomasine, the flight instinct coming to the fore. Felix knew it by glancing at her pale, strained face. She cocked her head, listening intently. They all did.

"Can you hear anything?" Tomasine asked, looking ready to bolt.

Felix moved closer, felt the faint trembling of her slender frame. Tenderness swamped him. She was such a tiny thing. Didn't she know he'd protect her with everything he had? They all would.

Footsteps sounded in the passage. Two sets.

"Saber wouldn't let in anyone who presented a danger," Leo said after noting Tomasine's worried face.

Emily nodded but Tomasine didn't seem convinced. Felix watched when her gaze sought out both Gina and Sylvie. Emily had found a book for Sylvie to color and Gina, who had become bored with their circular discussion, was helping with color selections. The closer the footsteps came, the more uneasy she became. Tomasine's breasts rose and fell with each jerky breath, her gaze darting around the room as if seeking a means of escape. She did this every time she entered a room even though the exits and entrances didn't change. It was an ingrained behavior and it chilled Felix to the bone. What the hell had happened to cause her such extreme wariness? He wished she'd confide in him.

Tomasine tensed at his side and leapt to her feet. She grabbed the nearest knife before glaring at the man. He was tall and powerfully built with tawny eyes and streaky blond hair. About

Saber's age, Felix decided, and there was something primal in his expression that hinted at shifter.

"What the hell are you doing here?" She turned her attention to Saber and glowered. "Check him for weapons." Her features went hard, her expression flat. Unforgiving. Her hand tightened on the knife. This man was part of her secret. She knew this shifter.

Felix gave him a careful look instead of the usual polite scan he reserved for a stranger. Jealousy followed swiftly as he wondered at the man's identity. Tomasine had said her husband was dead but what if he were still alive? What if she'd lied to him all along?

"I have," Saber said in a mild tone, his eyes on Tomasine. "His gun is in my office. I've searched him. He's unarmed now. You can put the knife down."

Felix narrowed his eyes at his brother. There was something...

"I mean you no harm, Your Majesty." The man bowed his head and waited.

"Your Majesty?" Felix repeated, full-out staring and unworried about the rudeness aspect now.

Leo gaped at Saber. "Who's he talking to?"

"Not me," Emily said. "And I know none of you guys have a drop of royal blood. That leaves Tomasine."

"Tomasine?" Shit, this was the secret she'd been keeping from them?

"I suppose Joseph sent you," Tomasine spat at the man. At a hard stare from Saber, she slapped the knife on the table. But not far enough away that she couldn't grab it again. "He's too much a coward to do the job himself."

"This is Lucas Kombu," Saber said. "Emily, perhaps he'd like a cup of coffee?"

"Take a seat," Felix said, indicating a seat at the far end of the table, away from Tomasine. It was more for Kombu's safety than Tomasine's. Felix saw the man nod at Emily and his gaze skirt over Sylvie and Gina but he didn't sit.

"Oh for goodness' sake." Tomasine plonked her butt on a chair and the man sat.

Protocol, Felix realized. Shit, he'd made love to royalty—probably a huge lapse in the protocol stakes. Would they want his head for the crime?

"This is Queen Augustus from the Tanzanian clan in Africa," Saber said, obviously deciding Tomasine wasn't going to tell them anything.

"That person no longer exists. I am Tomasine Brooks. What's with the sudden appearance in Middlemarch?" Her eyes narrowed on the man and Felix blinked at her imperious manner. Royalty and somehow he'd missed it. "Why are you confronting me face-to-face? Why didn't you just shoot me and hie back to Joseph to inform him you'd done the deed?" She paused and Felix could almost hear her brain ticking. "Did you have something to do with the body?"

"What about the mystery blonde?" Felix added, claiming the seat beside Tomasine and placing a proprietary hand on her shoulder.

The man—Lucas—blinked, his gaze on Felix for an instant before returning to Tomasine. "It was Robert. I don't know who killed him but I couldn't leave him with the authorities and let them discover he was a shifter. It would raise questions. I stole his body and disposed of it in the proper manner."

"What about the blonde?" Leo asked.

"You're fixated with the blonde lady," Gina said, her cheekiness earning her a glare from Tomasine. Gina shrugged unconcerned but Felix noticed her eavesdropping.

"None of us like surprises," Felix said. And wasn't that the truth. Bloody royalty. A queen. Where the hell did that leave him? Quick answer—in the same position he'd been in before Lucas had arrived. If Tomasine thought she could take off to parts unknown without him, she could bloody think again.

"We don't even know if she's a danger. She helped Sylvie avoid detection yesterday. She could have harmed her if that was her goal," Emily said.

Enough of the chitchat. Tomasine wanted real answers. "You haven't said why you're here." She used every ounce of her royal blood, lifting her chin in a haughty manner and arching her brows.

Lucas didn't hesitate. "Joseph is a dictator. He's taken over and a lot of us don't like the way things are going. It's worse than when Bernard was in power."

Dissent among the traitors—the surviving members of the clan. How apt. Then, a pang of regret softened her glower. She hadn't been strong enough to deal with Bernard, to make him see sense and rule with firmness yet kindness. After the mysterious deaths of her parents and older brother, she'd been thrust into a role before she was ready for it or received the correct training.

"I regret what happened with Bernard. I was too young and inexperienced to rule the clan on my parents' death. Bernard charmed me. By the time I realized I'd invited Joseph into the palace along with Bernard, it was too late."

Saber claimed a seat near Lucas and Leo took the empty one on the other side. Silent sentinels, willing to protect her should the need arise. In that moment, she realized she'd found a family, a real family, even though it wasn't what she'd been searching for. The knowledge warmed her, chipping away at the icy-cold demeanor she currently projected. Despite being unable to stay, she'd treasure the memory of their kindness.

"Joseph ordered the ethnic cleansing with Bernard's approval. They didn't like the half-breeds who had come into our clan group over the years." Lucas swallowed painfully. "They also used it as a way to rid themselves of their detractors."

"But the assassins killed everyone—men, women and children." Horror echoed in her voice. "They shot anyone who moved. It wasn't only clan members who spoke against them."

"They killed a whole clan of shifters?" Emily asked faintly.

"They killed everyone who lived in the savannah village. Bernard and I had stopped there on the way home from Kenya. Joseph had arranged the visit as a goodwill stop to try and halt the dissent among the clan. We went along with his suggestion, not knowing it was a deathtrap. Several of the elders tried to hustle me away. They managed to get Sylvie to safety but the elders with me were shot. One fell and knocked me off my feet. The other sheltered me and a flying bullet struck him. I lay under their bodies for hours, praying they wouldn't search and realize I was alive. I could smell the blood, the..." Tomasine broke off to swallow.

Memories crowded in on her, bringing back everything in frightening detail—the moans of the dying, the excited cries of the animals, the cruel laughter of the assassins and the smells.

"I...I waited until I thought they'd gone before I tried to move. God, the stench was horrible and the wild animals, the scavengers arrived." Tomasine shuddered, and when Felix drew her against his chest, she didn't struggle. Instead, she savored his quiet comfort. "When I crept out of cover, I found one of Joseph's minions trying to interfere with Gina. Joseph was very free with his wandering hands when Bernard wasn't present," Tomasine muttered. "Sly and nasty. Some of his men copied his example. I hit the scum over the head with a rock. We found Sylvie, salvaged what possessions we could and left. Joseph sent assassins after us. They've come close but so far we've managed to elude them. Until now."

Felix's arms tightened around her. "No one is going to get near either you or the girls."

Lucas cleared his throat. "That's what I wanted to tell you. I've sent a message to Joseph saying Robert and I found and disposed of you and your child. I said we found you in North Auckland. Kerikeri."

"Big of you." A flare of rage burned in Tomasine. "I hope you collect a big reward."

"I'm not going back," Lucas said with quiet dignity. "I intend to go to South America and start over. I don't want anything to do with Joseph's regime. Too many good people have died."

"Joseph isn't stupid," Tomasine said. "He'll want proof I'm dead."

"Yes, he does. I'm here to ask you to give me that proof." Lucas shifted uneasily, but went against tradition and maintained eye contact.

"My head?" Tomasine said, her tone dry.

Emily scowled. "I think I have a suitable platter."

A snort escaped Leo.

"Emily," Saber chided, looking at his mate.

"Well if he thinks we're going to turn Tomasine and the girls over to him, he needs his head seen to by a specialist," Emily snapped. "Do they think we're dummies?"

"If I send Joseph the royal seal, he'll believe me," Lucas said.

"The royal seal?" Felix said. "But if he has an official seal, won't that cement his position?"

"I don't have it." Even if she'd had the seal in her possession, Tomasine wasn't sure she would have handed it over. Yes, it might save her life and give the girls a shot at normal but it would also condemn the surviving members of her clan to a life of pure hell. "Bernard took it from me not long after we mated. He hid it—I don't know where since I never saw it again."

"Hell." Lucas drew a hand through his hair. "That's the only proof Joseph will accept. He'll pay people to make sure you don't surface. And I hate to tell you this but there's at least one assassin—a female—who hasn't checked in for some time."

Felix's hands tightened on her shoulders. "How long?"

Exactly what Tomasine wanted to know, especially with the mystery blonde woman appearing on the scene so often.

"Since the day of the attacks," Lucas said.

"What does she look like? Blonde?" Felix demanded before Tomasine had a chance to ask herself.

Her eyes narrowed when it hit her that the Mitchells had taken her under their wings. They were taking her relationship with Felix seriously and treating her as part of their family. Theirs to protect. The fit was uncomfortable, troubling and exhilarating at the same time. No one had cared for her in this way since her parents and brother had died. She cleared her throat and concentrated on Lucas and his motives. What if he was lying?

"She was tall, slim and had long dark hair. She was striking to look at yet still managed to blend into the background. Good at her job," Lucas added.

"That's comforting," Tomasine said.

"If she's an assassin, she probably is adept at disguises," Leo added.

Lucas shrugged. "We suspect she's dead because she hasn't checked in or touched the last payment we sent."

"But it might be the mystery blonde woman," Emily said, worry shading her voice.

Felix frowned. "Sylvie said the woman helped her. She's had the perfect opportunity if she'd meant to hurt either of you. Why would she hesitate if that's what she wants?"

"I agree with Felix," Saber said. "If she is an assassin, she's not in it for the money. She has another agenda. All we can do is watch and wait."

"Well, things just keep getting better." Tomasine lifted her chin and concentrated on remembering everything her mother had told her about being a royal. If she needed to keep one eye looking over her shoulder for the rest of her life, then so be it. She refused to go back.

"What does the seal look like?" Felix asked. "Would it be possible to make a good enough copy to fool Joseph?"

Tomasine shook her head. "It's made of solid gold and studded with tanzanite, a deep blue gemstone found in the clan lands. It would cost a fortune to reproduce and Joseph would call in experts to have it authenticated."

"Okay, as I see it, there's one more option you need to consider," Felix said. "Is there someone else you would consider suitable to rule your clan." He massaged the tight muscles at the back of her neck and she wanted to moan aloud. It felt that good. "Who is next in line?"

Tomasine frowned in deep concentration, sifting through the possibilities if she and Sylvie were taken out of the equation. She stilled before lifting her head to stare at Lucas. "Lucas is next in line."

"Which is why he's moving to South America," Saber said. "Have attempts been made on your life?"

Lucas nodded. "I don't like what's going on and made the mistake of sharing my doubts."

"Would you like to rule?" Tomasine couldn't contain her suspicion. It leaked into her words and showed as a furrow between her eyes. He *had* been on Joseph's side once.

"I'd prefer to breed polo horses in South America but I would make a better and fairer ruler than Joseph."

Tomasine sifted through what she knew of the male and had to concede. He'd never treated her badly and most of the clan had liked him. But she still had no idea how he could take over from Joseph. "That's a sensible solution for me, but how do I implement it with Joseph holding tight to the crown?"

"I have an idea. Put out a contract on Joseph," Felix said. "Use his own weapon against him and get rid of the despot."

Chapter 10

Operation Assassin

Tomasine stared at Felix for a long drawn-out moment. She closed her gaping mouth and offered a slow smile. "I like it."

"That's my girl," Felix said, hugging her before sitting back in his chair. He turned to Lucas. "How much will it cost? Can you arrange it for us?"

"I can arrange it." Lucas's frown was troubled. "But it will be expensive. Joseph is well protected and it may take time. If Joseph is eliminated, you can take back power and rule," he added.

"I don't want that—not for me or for Sylvie. Besides the remaining clan members are as rotten as Joseph." Her eyes narrowed on Lucas and he returned her gaze without flinching.

"How much money?" asked Saber.

The figure Lucas named made Tomasine blink in shock. "There's no way I can raise that sort of money. God, no wonder so many of the clan is suffering. Joseph must be bleeding the clan resources dry in his determination for absolute rule."

"I have a little I can contribute," Lucas said.

"We will contribute too," Saber said.

"Of course we will," Emily said, reaching over the table to cover Tomasine's hand with her own. "Wow, to think I didn't know any of this shifter stuff went on before. My eyes are open now."

Tomasine didn't know what to say. A suspicious moistness welled and blurred her vision. She blinked but it made the condition worse.

"And meanwhile, you and I and the girls will go to live at Saul's uncle's station. I can help with work on the farm while you can write your articles and help out with the home schooling if you want."

Tomasine glanced at Felix, taking in his stern face and dark good looks. "I..." She swallowed and tried again, her heart rate double timing. It was all she'd ever wanted. Security and a family. A man who loved her. It was hers for the taking if she had the courage to say yes. She took a deep breath. "I...okay."

Felix tugged her chair around so she faced him. He gripped her shoulders and stared intently into her eyes. "Really?"

A slow and sexy smile curved across her lips and dug into her cheeks. She knew he was asking for more than her agreement to live at the secluded station. Tomasine nodded but didn't want any misconceptions from anyone. "I will be your mate and become Tomasine Mitchell."

Felix hauled Tomasine to her feet and yanked her into his arms. Seconds later his mouth slammed down on hers. There was a clash of teeth before their mouths aligned and then it was absolutely perfect. She put everything she had into the kiss while thanking the fates for arranging their collision outside the post office.

Gradually the sound of applause registered and Tomasine pulled away from Felix. To her consternation, a blush heated her cheeks.

"Are you sure, Majesty?" Lucas asked.

"Queen Augustus no longer exists. Call me Tomasine, and yes, I'm very sure." She bowed her head then raised it, well aware of the weight that had disappeared from her shoulders.

"This calls for champagne," Saber said.

"But it's still early," Emily protested.

"I don't care." Saber stalked to the fridge and pulled out a bottle. He opened it efficiently and Emily produced glasses.

"He's been hoarding that bottle since he first thought up the harebrained scheme to marry off all of us," Felix said. "Let him have a moment to gloat."

Saber nodded and started filling the glasses. A pleased grin wreathed his lips. "Damn straight," he said. "One down and three to go."

It was late when Felix ushered Tomasine into their bedroom.

"This is your last chance to change your mind," she said.

Felix snorted. "Isn't that my line?"

"Not in this case. I'm the one with assassins on my tail. I don't want you to have regrets later."

He cupped her face in his big hands. "Tomasine, I'm not going anywhere. I love you."

"Are you sure we'll be safe on the station?"

"Yeah. I wouldn't suggest it otherwise." Felix brushed a lock of hair off her face. "We have more important things to do."

"Sex." Tomasine chewed on her bottom lip to stop throwing herself at him. She didn't want to appear too eager. Difficult given the way her breasts rubbed against her bra, her nipples sensitive and needy for his touch, his mouth.

"Damn right." Felix peered at her, touching his hand to her forehead. "You okay? You're feeling a bit hot even for a shifter."

Hot. That was an understatement. Ever since she'd said yes, her body had hijacked her, sending "hurry and mate messages" to her brain. Goose bumps prickled across her arms and legs and each delicate brush of his fingers brought another wave of arousal to dampen her panties. "I'm fine." A big fat lie. "No, I'm not," she said, determined to have truth between them now instead of secrets. The driving needs of her body had blindsided her a little, taking her unawares since she'd never felt this way with Bernard. Never.

"What's wrong?"

"Nothing sleep won't cure."

"Sleep. Right. Let's get you to bed then."

"Yes please," she purred.

Felix's eyes gleamed with comprehension. "Better take off your clothes. Don't want you getting too hot."

Tomasine bit back a laugh. "That might be best." She stood still while he unbuttoned her pink shirt. He seemed to do lots of touching—unnecessary contact in her opinion and it made her ultra aware of her body, the way her clothes fitted to her form. Finally, he smoothed her shirt from her shoulders, baring her over-heated flesh to his gaze. She smiled up at him and licked her lips with careful precision.

Felix growled at the back of his throat and her smile heated to a grin. Loving Felix was fun. He was a caring, generous lover who reveled in her pleasure.

His knuckle grazed the curve of one breast and a shiver worked through her.

"Can you go any slower?"

"I can," he said. "Do you want to have more children?"

Tomasine thought for a second. A child or children with dark hair and green eyes like Felix. Children who made discipline impossible because their killer grins caused her to go soft and gooey inside. Siblings for Sylvie and Gina.

"Yes." Her heart did a quick pitter-patter on seeing the elation in his eyes. "I would like your children as soon as we know it is safe."

"I don't want to wait," he whispered, tracing his thumb across her lips. The heat in his eyes brought a shudder of awareness, of wanting and passionate need. "We're safe. I promise nothing will happen to you or the girls. We won't let anything go wrong."

Tomasine believed him. Having Felix around and knowing other shifters were watching out for them brought a lump to her throat. She opened her mouth and sucked his thumb inside. She rasped her tongue across his skin in a seductive move, bathing the tip of his thumb. She ran her tongue into the gap between his fingernail and thumb tip.

Felix pulled away with a hiss. He stepped back from her and started to unbutton his shirt. "Undress," he ordered in a tight voice. "Now."

Tomasine smirked, knowing she'd pushed him with that little act. It was good to know he was as strung out as her, that he wanted her so much. Arousing as hell. She reached behind her back to flick her bra open and stripped it down her arms, tossing the garment aside. She wriggled out of her jeans and panties, giving an extra seductive sway of her hips. A masculine groan told her he'd stopped to watch her strip. She stepped from the last of her clothing and shimmied her shoulders. Her breasts jiggled. Yes! A successful attempt to gain his full attention.

She suppressed a chuckle and said in an innocent tone, "You're not getting ready for bed now?"

"No," he said in a dark voice as he shucked his underwear. "I don't intend to sleep much tonight."

Her brows shot up in an expression of innocence while she suppressed the need to snigger. "Do tell."

"I'm going to make love to my mate." He prowled toward her with clear intent.

Tomasine backed up until the bed stopped farther retreat. She giggled. "Come get me."

"I intend to." His green eyes glowed, dark and mysterious, and they contained passion, so much stormy passion, for her.

Her laughter fell away, replaced by urgency. She leaned closer, and dragged the tips of her breasts across his broad chest. A quick glance caught his flash of raw need.

He grunted when she rubbed against his groin and moved a fraction. "Now is not the time to tease, not when my control is hanging by a sliver."

Tomasine understood what he meant. She slid her tongue across her canines and found them partially extended. "Kiss me. Please."

"Yeah. I can do that. I need to touch." His laugh emerged ragged and his hand trembled when he reached to cup her jaw. "Hell, my skin is prickling like it does at the start of the change." He didn't give her a chance to respond. His mouth settled on hers, taking. Demanding a response. She opened for him and he savored the faint taste of coffee and the brandy they'd drunk after the celebratory dinner Emily had cooked for them. The underlying sweetness was pure Tomasine.

Addictive. *His*.

Their tongues slid together with the faint rasping characteristic of shifters. Her canines had lengthened, as had his, bringing lurking danger from sharp teeth. But he didn't hesitate, crowding closer, his hand tangling in the hair at her nape. God, he loved this woman. In his mind, she was his mate already. All he needed was to make her his in fact. With a quick move, he scooped Tomasine off her feet and placed her in the middle of the mattress.

Before she could move, he covered her with his body, pressing her down so she couldn't move. Smirking, he stared deep into her eyes before scanning her face and lingering on her lips. "I have you. Now what are you going to do?"

"Love you," she said.

Her words struck like a sucker punch. They floored him with their simplicity and tugged at every one of his emotions. *Love*. Hell, that was easy with Tomasine. And knowing she loved him in return—that was his biggest reward.

Felix kissed her again and stretched against her in a full body rub. When she purred, he grinned and set about exploring her curves. He nuzzled behind her ear and gave in to temptation and licked. One long lick across luscious, silky skin. He inhaled the scent of her excitement along with the delicate bouquet of wildflowers and grasses. He heard the racing of her heart and a ripple of awareness that preceded the shift to cat shot the length of his body.

His swollen cock jerked, the sensitive head rubbing against her flesh. Felix controlled the change, letting his body hover on the fringe instead.

"I can hear the rush of blood through your veins. The beat of your heart," she murmured.

"I know. I wanted to go slow this time, sweetheart. I can't." Felix nuzzled the plump curve of one breast and breathed moist, warm air across the tip.

"Slow is for later," she whispered. "Once we've burned away the mating lust." Her eyes shone golden and more catlike than he'd seen them before. A queen. He, Felix Mitchell, was mating with royalty.

"You know, I've never done it with royalty before."

Tomasine made a scoffing noise. "Yes, you have. Yesterday. And the day before that."

"Yeah, but I didn't know I was doing it with a queen."

"I'm the same shifter I was before. Being royal doesn't make a better person," she said in a stiff voice.

Felix knew he'd pressed a hot button for her. Her royal blood had brought problems, things they couldn't sweep under the nearest pile of schist and forget.

"Do you want to rule?" she demanded. "There won't be much left. Traitors and debts most likely. A raft of problems."

"Me?" Felix asked in clear horror. "Hell no! I want to live on the land and farm like my forebears. I don't want to rule over a clan and worry about them. All I want is a quiet life with you and the girls. Besides, if you think I'm getting in one of those metal tubes and flying through the sky, you can bloody think again. Shifters weren't made to fly."

"What if I decided to return to Africa and take control of the remains of the clan resources?" Tomasine asked.

The question drew Felix up short. As much as he disliked flying, he didn't intend to lose Tomasine now that he'd found her. He took a deep breath and smoothed the hair away from her face. "I guess I'd have to organize a passage on a cruise ship." Not that he liked the thought of being on the ocean much better but they were discussing Tomasine. His mate. Where she went so did he.

"Relax. You're safe." Her golden eyes twinkled at him. "I like New Zealand. I'm not going anywhere."

The wretch had been teasing. Felix growled and stopped fighting the change as he had been. A light coating of dark hair formed on his chest.

"Ohh," Tomasine cooed, smoothing her hand across the smooth pelt.

"Remember what I said about teasing?"

She contained her merriment but he saw it in her beautiful eyes. "Traditional?"

"Yeah. Please." Felix stroked her cheek with his strong fingers.

"Are you going to let me bite you?"

"Of course. I want a true mating." He scrutinized her before letting his breath ease out in enlightenment. "Your husband mated with you to ensure your cooperation but wouldn't allow you the same power over him." Bastard. No wonder she'd been so wary.

"A true mating. Really?"

"Nothing else will do." Felix kissed her and ran his tongue over her teeth. Her canines were pronounced. Sharp. He lifted his head. "You will mark me first." The minute he'd said the words, he knew he'd done the right thing. An expression of awe and blinding love seared across her face and it humbled him.

"Felix, I love you," she whispered, her fingers massaging the fleshy part of his shoulder, the place she'd mark.

"I know it, sweetheart." His cock jerked hard in reaction and it seemed as if every bit of blood in his body crowded into his groin. His skin prickled and more dark hair formed on his arms, legs and torso. A shimmer of golden light glowed around him and the light coating of hair started to flash.

With serious intent written on every inch of her face, she reached up and licked across the fleshy part where shoulder and neck met. Her tongue was rough and abrasive and it sent desire pumping through him. Every one of his senses intensified, working overtime and bombarding him with messages of passion and sex and loving. He swallowed, wallowing in the carnal images flickering through him like a blockbuster movie. Tomasine sighed and licked again, then without warning, she bit down. For an instant, he felt her sharp canines pricking into his flesh then there was nothing but blinding-white pleasure. The enzymes in her saliva mixed with his blood and each swathe of her tongue brought a wave of sensation to his cock and balls. Painfully tight and needy, the slit at the end of his cock oozed pre-cum.

Finally, she pulled away. A bead of blood welled at the spot she'd bitten, and he watched her lick it away. The delicate flicker of her tongue pushed past his control.

Felix grabbed Tomasine and flipped her over on her belly. She didn't panic at his abrupt move but glanced over her shoulder. Her sultry gaze and the faint golden luminosity around her petite body severed the last of his control. Felix arranged her on hands and knees and paused to admire her curvy body, presented for him. Felix fought the primal demand to surge between her legs and clamp down with his teeth.

Despite the urgency thrumming through him, he wanted this to be an occasion they'd remember with fondness, with happy memories, and most of all with blinding satisfaction. His eyes caressed every part of her while the sound of her racing pulse sought to distract, to make him hurry.

He licked down her spine, tasting her skin and seeing if he could drive her heart rate even higher. The golden glow bathed them both and he noticed Tomasine was exhibiting signs of partial change as well. Felix cupped the firm globes of her butt and widened her stance to catch a glimpse of her pussy. He closed his eyes for an instant. God. He was a lucky man. Taking his cock in one hand, he guided it the length of her cleft, stopping just short of her clit.

Tomasine concentrated on breathing and holding her shape. She'd never felt so turned on, so needy before. And the moment when she'd bitten into his flesh and marked him—she shuddered at the remembered pleasure. The taste of him played through her memory again. A tight sensation in her throat caused her to swallow. Twice. He probed her entrance, smoothing her arousal juices upward and teasing across her puckered rosette. A moan escaped her and he chuckled—a dark sound, one of a man struggling for control, and she loved knowing she could make him this way.

Without warning, he pushed deep with one seamless thrust. Tomasine thought about a condom before discarding the thought. She wanted Felix's child. Together they would keep their children safe.

She felt his cock throbbing deep inside her. He seemed bigger, larger than usual, and despite her arousal, she struggled to take him. The thin line between pleasure and pain blurred, coalescing before turning to pure ecstasy. He nuzzled her neck and her heart seemed to stop.

Bite me.

She wanted it so bad, needed it as much as her next breath. Tomasine needed to know he desired her as much as she hungered for him. *Please, bite me.*

He licked, the rough and abrasive feel of his tongue lashing every pleasure point. "Please," she gasped. She pleaded. She demanded. "*Please.*"

When she glanced over her shoulder, she saw he was as close to losing control as she. With the golden luminosity around him, he looked mystical. Powerful.

Her mate.

He withdrew before smoothly pushing his cock deep again. They both sighed and a streak of pleasure shot through her.

"Are you ready?" Felix asked, his voice tight. Tense.

"Ready and impatient."

He gave a bark of laughter. "Can't have that."

"No."

Felix nibbled at the spot where her neck and shoulder met, the exact place where she'd marked him. The play of his teeth across her flesh sent a ripple through her, a clenching of her channel. He groaned, the throbbing hardness of him filling her impossibly full. His talented fingers slipped along her folds and he strummed her swollen clit at the same instant he bit down. Fiery pleasure lashed her, even better than when she'd bitten him and tasted his blood welling in her mouth. She shuddered helplessly, the bite acting as an avalanche, sweeping her away, pushing her into climax. She shattered in convulsive waves, felt his explosive contractions when he came and the delicate lap of his rough tongue as he encouraged the mixing of enzymes between them.

"Felix."

He lifted his head and withdrew from her body in one quick move. Before she knew it, she was in his protective arms. The golden glow faded and she was vaguely aware of her skin prickling and her body retreating to human.

"Tomasine." His voice held a wealth of emotion as he kissed her lingeringly. "My mate." He smoothed her tangled hair from her face, his green eyes glowing with love.

"Yes." And he was hers. The emotion was real—she experienced it with every particle of her body. It was as if physical chains and locks had snapped into place, so strong was the sense of knowing, of belonging. "I love you, my mate." And that was true as well. She loved him unconditionally. Somehow in all the turbulence, she'd found the one man—a shifter male—who made her whole.

W ant a hint about what comes next? Turn the page to read a new bonus chapter featuring Saber Mitchell and the members of the Feline Council and also an excerpt from *My Assassin*, the next book in the Middlemarch Shifters series.

Chapter 11

Bonus Chapter

Mitchell Farm, Middlemarch, New Zealand

Feline Shapeshifter Council Meeting.

Present: Saber Mitchell, Sid Blackburn, Kenneth Nesbitt, Agnes Paisley, Valerie McClintock, Benjamin Urquart

"A queen. Felix has m-mated with a queen." Agnes gaped at Saber, her mouth opening and closing. "Who would've guessed? Such a n-naughty child, he was. You're pulling my leg."

"Nope. We'll have to bow to him now." Saber fought to contain his grin and failed. He'd never seen Agnes stutter before.

"Get away with you, lad." Sid winked before sobering. "Given the circumstances, we must watch for strangers. I think we should call a shifter meeting to stress how dangerous it could be if someone speaks to the wrong person."

Valerie nodded. "I agree. We must face the risks."

"Felix and Tomasine are leaving to stay with Saul's uncle until we're certain the danger is past, but we're putting out the story they're going to Auckland. We've put a hit out on Joseph, the man behind the death attempts on Tomasine and her daughters."

Silence greeted his words—the first time this lot appeared at a loss for words in Saber's memory.

"I see." Valerie removed her glasses and pulled a handkerchief out of her handbag to clean the lenses. The scent of lavender filled the air. "Was that necessary?"

"We couldn't think of an alternative to halt Joseph Magumbo. He's responsible for killing most of Tomasine's clan. Men, women and children."

"Children too?" Kenneth asked, filling the shocked silence.

Saber nodded. "Felix refused to let Tomasine leave Middlemarch without him, and offering to pay for a hit seemed the only way. Lucas, Tomasine's cousin, is helping us finance the deal. He says he'll repay us once he seizes control of the clan."

"Lad, do you trust him?" Sid asked.

Saber rose to get a fresh pot of coffee from the kitchen and returned. "I'm undecided. He seems determined, but we won't know for some time. He approached us. He knew Tomasine's location. He could've bade his time and killed her. Instead, he knocked on our door and allowed me to search him. More coffee?"

"Thank you," Benjamin said.

Several mugs were shunted in his direction and Saber poured the refills.

"We'll call the meeting," Kenneth said. "Make sure everyone is aware of the problem and spell out what action they need to take if they see anyone suspicious."

"Agreed," Agnes said.

The others nodded in agreement.

"Speaking of strangers," Saber said. "My cousin Sam mentioned that two of his friends intend to visit the area. They want to start a security business and are searching for premises. One is a feline shifter and the other a werewolf. I'll call Sam back and make sure I have a description and ask them to let us know when they'll arrive."

"What sort of premises?" Benjamin asked.

"I don't know," Saber said. "What is on the agenda for this afternoon?"

Agnes tapped her pen against the committee book. "We made a small profit on the woolshed dance. The sales of the padlocks are going well, and we're getting tourists coming to photograph our fence. It's—"

"Someone has started hanging bras on the fence," Valerie interrupted. "I removed three yesterday, and today when I drove past, there were at least half a dozen hanging alongside the padlocks."

Kenneth smirked as he picked up a date scone and applied himself to adding jam and cream. "More than that now. I watched a busload of tourists pull up before I drove here. Several of the girls whipped off their bras and added them."

"We need a sign," Agnes said.

Sid winked at Saber. "I have a better idea. Why don't we add an honesty box and a sign? Let them have their fun. Make a section of the fence available for bras and appoint someone to remove them once a week."

"No! Definitely not," Agnes said, her pen *tap, tap, tapping* on her book.

"Don't think Erin, your granddaughter, agrees," Benjamin said. "I saw her and her friends tie their bras on the fence myself."

Valerie chortled, spluttering coffee over the table. She wiped it with her hand, still smirking at the news.

"I wouldn't laugh too hard, Valerie." Ben's eyes took on a feline glint. "Your granddaughter's bra is flying in the breeze beside Erin's."

"Never," Valerie said, aghast.

Benjamin's green eyes gleamed greener and brighter and his shoulders shook with merriment.

The two feline women shared a panicked glance, and Saber hid his grin with his coffee mug.

"Marry them off," Kenneth announced, which caused all the men to cackle. "That will keep them out of mischief. Now that the sports field is completed and the first rugby game is in two weeks, why don't we hold a social?"

"We could do that," Saber said, feeling in charity with Kenneth. It hadn't been too long ago when he and his brothers were in the council firing line. "Invite the other team and charge a small admission. But Emily had a couple of good ideas. One is to start a monthly craft fair. She suggests we invite people to sell their wares and charge them for a table on which to sell their crafts or produce. Gradually, this will bring more people into the town. She says it might be slow at first but as the word spreads, more people would visit. She also suggested that the Scouts or one of the other groups be in charge of a sausage sizzle and tea or coffee to raise funds."

Agnes clapped her hands together in delight. "Oh, what good ideas. Your mate is such a treasure."

Saber glanced around the table and saw the other council members nodding in agreement. While pleased, anticipation swirled within him. He could hardly wait to tell them Emily's second idea. "That's the first idea."

Sid beamed. "There's more, lad?"

"Yes." A chortle escaped Saber. "You know what zombies are?"

Agnes straightened, the nostrils of her thin nose flaring in alarm. She exchanged a glance with Valerie, then shifted her focus back to Saber. "You're not telling us they're real? I believe they eat brains."

Saber barked out a laugh, and Benjamin and Sid echoed his merriment. "No, they're fictional."

Valerie shuddered and patted the left side of her chest in audible thumps. "Thank goodness."

Kenneth took a bite of his scone and swallowed. "What about zombies?"

"Since they're so popular, Emily suggested we set up a zombie run." He held up his hand to halt questions. "What happens is we organize people to dress up as zombies and station them along a running course. Then, we charge participants to run the course and give prizes for those who manage to get past the zombies without getting captured. We also give out prizes for the best costumes."

Agnes sniffed. "It sounds silly."

"But it will bring in young people," Sid said thoughtfully. "That is our main purpose. Every function we organize needs to bring in prospective mates."

"Will women want to do this?" Valerie sounded doubtful.

"Simple." Saber set down his coffee mug. "The runners operate in a team. Put it in the rules that they need to have a fifty-fifty split of sexes."

Agnes frowned. "You really think this will attract youngsters?"

"Yes," Saber said.

"We could organize a zombie week in town. Maybe Emily could make zombie cupcakes or something to go with the theme. We could have a movie night at the hall. The pub could invent a zombie drink," Kenneth said, full of enthusiasm.

"We could," Valerie said slowly, "ask the local community for suggestions of events to hold during our zombie theme week."

"We'll hit the internet," Benjamin said. "I like the idea, lad. It's different and unique. Bound to draw the right sort of attention to the town." He sent a sly glance in Valerie and Agnes's direction. "Maybe we can get those granddaughters of yours married off. They're close to going off the rails."

"Humph," Valerie said.

Agnes didn't comment, although her cheeks went pink.

Sid leaned back in his chair. "I like the idea too. Both the craft fair and the zombie run and theme week. Let's think about it this week and bring our suggestions for our next meeting."

"Works for me," Kenneth said.

"I think we can start making decisions on the craft market now," Saber said. "We can use the school hall. Emily said indoors would work best in case of bad weather. I suggest we put out the word to those interested and set a date for next month. Anyone can buy a table for twenty dollars and sell their produce or crafts."

"I'll speak to the school board," Agnes said.

"I'll liaise with you and take care of publicity," Kenneth offered.

"Tell the school board we'll give them half of the table fees," Sid said. "That is fair since we're using their hall."

The front door opened and childish laughter rippled through the house. Small feet thundered across the floor in their direction.

"Uncle Saber! We're home. Aunty Emily let me make cupcakes while Felix and Mum went for a walk," Sylvie said.

Saber grinned, imagining what his brother and new mate had got up to during their "walk". He knew how it felt to have a mate, the way the blood ran hot. "That's great, Sylvie."

Tomasine and Felix appeared in the doorway.

"Sylvie," Tomasine chided. "Uncle Saber is busy."

"It's all right. We're almost done," Agnes said, beaming at them all.

Saber almost snorted, but held it in. He was happy for his brother.

"Congratulations," Sid said and the others echoed the sentiment.

"Sorry to interrupt. We'll let you finish up," Felix said and ushered his youngest daughter and new mate from the room.

Saber heard a familiar vehicle and pleasure swept him. Emily was home. "Are we all decided?" Time to hurry the council members along.

"Yes," Sid said. "We're old hands at dances and socials, so we'll get that underway for the opening of the sports field. We'll research this zombie thing and Agnes can get started on the craft angle."

Kenneth stood and Saber wanted to cheer, since all the others rose too, ready to depart.

Emily joined him and they waved off the council. "That was a quick meeting. Did they like my ideas?"

Saber took her hand, entwining their fingers. "It's still nice out. Why don't I tell you all about it while we go for a walk?"

Emily stood on tiptoe and kissed his cheek. "We could get up to lots of mischief during a walk."

"Exactly, my plan."

And laughing, Saber and his mate walked away from the house with misbehavior on their minds. An excellent way to end the afternoon.

Excerpt: My Assassin

T he bastard was out there.

Like a predator, Isabella Black suspected he stalked his prey, prepared to pounce at the first opportunity. The same instinct that had led her to come outside and scout the vicinity told her he skulked in the shadows, hidden out of sight, waiting with patience.

With tension swirling in her stomach, she scanned the hills and rocky outcrops, resisting the urge to stomp back and forth in a show of frustration. She loathed this situation. It pushed her temper from calm to uncertain, which wasn't good for someone in her line of work. Her breath escaped in an impatient hiss.

At least the target remained safe, stashed in a secure house on an isolated farm. Felix Mitchell guarded his new family with determination and love. *As it should be*. He was an honorable man and perfect for Tomasine.

Isabella swiveled to scan the main road dissecting the small township of Middlemarch. The breeze ruffled her shoulder-length blonde hair, and she brushed it off her face with an impatient hand. She reached for the case holding her high-powered rifle. Assembling the weapon by touch, she loaded it, then held the rifle in her hands. Eyes watchful, she scanned her surroundings.

No strangers.

Not a thing out of the ordinary.

Then a flash of light, to the right of a leaning pine, caught her attention.

"Move again. Let me get a glimpse of you."

With infinite resolve, she waited until she caught the outline of a figure picking his way across the hill, slinking from rock to tree.

"That's it," she crooned, fingers flexing around her rifle. She watched him in her telescopic sight, noted his familiar features. One of Mika's cronies. Even if she hadn't recognized him, the weapon he carried gave away his purpose.

The man meant business.

Kill or be killed.

She aimed until his face lined up in the crosshairs of her sight and squeezed the trigger, feeling not a trace of remorse.

He fell, remained still.

A quick check ensured no one had witnessed the hit. Not a soul stirred, which wasn't unusual around Middlemarch since it was a country town. Isabella crept closer, needing to confirm his death for peace of mind. She watched the body up on the hill, frowned at his motionless form. A few seconds later, she slid through the darkness, approaching with caution. When he still didn't stir, she nudged him with her foot, stooped to check his pulse.

Dead.

She eyed him, the blood around his head and couldn't be sorry. A sleaze. The man enjoyed making his victims suffer, especially the women. Didn't matter how old, they experienced his special brand of torture.

"What the hell am I going to do with you now?" It wasn't as if she could leave him. Another body. Questions would be raised, but forensics wouldn't tie her to him, not even the bullets since she'd used her last African-bought bullet to do the deed.

Isabella went through his pockets and after careful consideration left his identification. He had a record and was no loss, although the local police might connect his body to the last suspicious death in Middlemarch. With a final visual check, she scooped up his weapons and retreated.

With the ease of practice, she packed up her rifle, strode to her bike. After stashing her weapon bag on the back and fastening her black helmet beneath her chin, she straddled the machine and started it with a throaty roar. She coasted down the hill, thoughts turbulent and worrying.

Another mercenary eliminated, which left Mika wandering the countryside. Time to flush him from hiding. As far as she knew, he was the last assassin after Tomasine. Originally, there had been eight. Over the years Isabella had taken care of the rest, but Mika was more determined than most—skilled and experienced.

A scowl twisted her lips. There was always the possibility Joseph had hired another batch of mercenaries to track

Tomasine and assassinate her. She had experience with despots. They never felt secure until every single enemy lay dead in their graves. Their propensity for paranoia kept them alive.

Her features twisted into a full-on snarl. This self-imposed guard duty might continue for years, and her chances of an ordinary life...

"Shit." An unaccustomed burn at the back of her eyes made her blink, and she gritted her teeth so hard it hurt. The sliver of pain centered her, brought focus. A professional, she'd keep going until the job ended in a satisfactory manner.

No matter how long it took.

Isabella rode out of town toward Dunedin and the cottage she'd rented as a base, a place where she could relax and be herself. Far enough out of Middlemarch to avoid investigation by the Mitchells, their friends and neighbors, yet close enough for her to keep an eye on events as they unfolded.

Half an hour later, she pulled into a long driveway and sped along the tree-lined track leading to her rented cottage. Out of sight of the main road, she came to a halt and switched off the ignition. The silence always amazed her. Apart from the tweet of birds and the contented bleats from the flock of sheep in the neighboring paddock, a sense of isolation persisted. Weird how she now loved the countryside around Middlemarch. Even the frigid winter temperatures didn't faze her these days. The town had become home, drilling into her heart—

Isabella broke off the thought and chuckled—rich amusement of the type to attract masculine attention. "Double damn," she muttered as her traitorous body shot to full alert and the image of a man crept into her mind. Thinking about males wasn't the ideal way to go into a hunt. Thinking about a *particular* male rated as suicide.

Is Isabella gonna get her man? Grab a copy of My Assassin to find out!

Also By Shelley

Middlemarch Gathering
My Highland Mate
My Highland Fling

Middlemarch Capture
Snared by Saber
Favored by Felix
Lost with Leo
Spellbound with Sly
Journey with Joe
Star-Crossed with Scarlett

About Author

USA Today bestselling author Shelley Munro lives in Auckland, the City of Sails, with her husband and a cheeky Jack Russell/mystery breed dog.

Typical New Zealanders, Shelley and her husband left home for their big OE soon after they married (translation of New Zealand speak - big overseas experience). A twelve-month-long adventure lengthened to six years of roaming the world. Enduring memories include being almost sat on by a mountain gorilla in Rwanda, lazing on white sandy beaches in India, whale watching in Alaska, searching for leprechauns in Ireland, and dealing with ghosts in an English pub.

While travel is still a big attraction, these days Shelley is most likely found in front of her computer following another love - that of writing stories of contemporary and paranormal romance and adventure. Other interests include watching rugby (strictly for research purposes), cycling, playing croquet and the ukelele, and curling up with an enjoyable book.

Visit Shelley at her Website

SHELLEY MUNRO

www.shelleymunro.com

Join Shelley's Newsletter www.shelleymunro.com/newsletter

Visit Shelley's Facebook page
www.facebook.com/ShelleyMunroAuthor

Follow Shelley at Bookbub
www.bookbub.com/authors/shelley-munro

Ingram Content Group UK Ltd.
Milton Keynes UK
UKHW040726080323
418175UK00004B/490

9 781991 063038